Advertising Media Volume 186

FEATURE SPOTLIGHT

This Week in Advertising...

The Adman:
Ash Williams

His New Campaign:
Truth serum. When you have to discover what's real...by whatever means necessary.

We've been wondering what's been going on with Ash Williams. Maddox Communications' CFO has always been controlled and on his game. But lately he's become very distracted, almost as if he were missing something. Could it have been a woman? Perhaps the very same woman who is now living in Ash's home? His fiancée...?

How is it possible that one of the most eligible bachelors in San Francisco is engaged and no one suspected a thing? We've all seen how Ash has discarded one woman after another, never willing to be "shackled" for long. So why is this mystery woman now wearing his ring, having no memory of how or *why* the millionaire proposed?

Dear Reader,

Welcome to book four of the KINGS OF THE BOARDROOM series, the story of CFO Ash Williams and his mistress, Melody Trent. Or is she his fiancée? I guess you'll just have to read to find out!

There is nothing more lethal than a man with power who is out for revenge. Especially one who is too stubborn to consider that he might be wrong. Ash is determined to make Melody pay for betraying him. But it's tough to be angry with someone recovering from a nearly critical brain injury. And even harder to hold her responsible for things she can't remember doing. She's not the person she was before the accident. He has to wonder if he's finally seeing the real Melody, not the carbon-copy mistress she thought he wanted her to be.

She nearly died, and she spent weeks in a coma, but Melody Trent refuses to let her guard down and play the victim, and she's wary of this steamy man who claims to be her fiancé. His story checks out, and he's playing the part of the devoted companion convincingly, but she can't shake the feeling he's hiding something. What was she doing in Texas without him, and why was she carrying four thousand dollars in her purse?

Melody wants answers, but Ash is determined to keep their past a secret. Now that he's let himself fall for her, her memories are the one thing that could tear them apart.

Writing their story was exhilarating and heartbreaking and sometimes downright confusing! But their journey was a rewarding one.

I hope you enjoy it!

Best,

Michelle

MICHELLE CELMER

MONEY MAN'S FIANCÉE NEGOTIATION

Silhouette
Desire

Published by Silhouette Books
America's Publisher of Contemporary Romance

Special thanks and acknowledgment to Michelle Celmer for her contribution to the KINGS OF THE BOARDROOM miniseries.

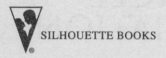 SILHOUETTE BOOKS

Recycling programs for this product may not exist in your area.

ISBN-13: 978-0-373-73019-3

MONEY MAN'S FIANCÉE NEGOTIATION

Books by Michelle Celmer

Silhouette Desire

Playing by the Baby Rules #1566
The Seduction Request #1626
Bedroom Secrets #1656
Round-the-Clock Temptation #1683
House Calls #1703
The Millionaire's Pregnant Mistress #1739
The Secretary's Secret #1774
Best Man's Conquest #1799
The King's Convenient Bride #1876
The Illegitimate Prince's Baby #1877
An Affair with the Princess #1900
The Duke's Boardroom Affair #1919
Royal Seducer #1951
The Oilman's Baby Bargain #1970
Christmas with the Prince #1979
Money Man's Fiancée Negotiation #2006

*Royal Seductions

MICHELLE CELMER

Bestselling author Michelle Celmer lives in southeastern Michigan with her husband, their three children, two dogs and two cats. When she's not writing or busy being a mom, you can find her in the garden or curled up with a romance novel. And if you twist her arm really hard you can usually persuade her into a day of power shopping.

Michelle loves to hear from readers. Visit her Web site, www.michellecelmer.com, or write her at P.O. Box 300, Clawson, MI 48017.

To the ladies of Sister Night:
Karen, Janet, Susie, Toni and Cora.

Prologue

February

Melody Trent shoved clothes into a suitcase feeling a sense of urgency that was totally without merit. Ash wouldn't be back until late. He'd been working longer and longer hours lately. Spending less and less time with her. Honestly, she would be surprised if it didn't take a few days before he even noticed she was gone.

Emotion welled up in her throat and tears stung her eyes. She bit down hard on the inside of her cheek and took a deep, calming breath. It had to be hormones because she had never been a crier.

She would love to be able to blame her mother and her revolving bedroom door for this. She would like to think that she'd stayed with Ash for three years because her mother's longest marriage—and there were five in total—barely lasted nine months. She wanted to be different from her mother, better than her, and look at the mess it had gotten her into.

She looked over at the photo on the dresser of her and her mother. It was the only one Mel had of them together. She was thirteen, with the body of a ten-year-old. Scrawny, skinny and awkward, standing next to her voluptuous, beautiful mother. No wonder she'd felt so insignificant, so invisible. It wasn't until college, when she shared an apartment with another student who worked part-time as a personal fitness trainer, that she finally started looking like a woman. It took vigorous daily workouts and relentless weight training, but she finally had curves to speak of, and within a year men began noticing her and asking her out.

Her body was the bait, and sex the addiction that kept them coming around, that kept them interested, because what other reason would a man have to be with someone like her? She was smart, but in her own opinion not very pretty. She was content to sit at home and study, or read a good novel, when her peers only wanted to party.

That was why she and Ash had always worked so well. She was able to go to law school, and do all the other things she enjoyed, and never worry about how the rent would get paid, or where she would find money for her next meal. He took care of her financially, and in return all she had to do was take care of everything else. And the truth was, she didn't mind the cooking and cleaning and laundry. She'd been doing it nearly her whole life, as her mother had never taken an interest in anything domestic—God forbid she break a nail.

And of course part of the package was keeping him sexually satisfied, and at that she was a master. Only lately, the past six months or so, she could feel him pulling away from her. When they made love she felt as though his mind was somewhere else. No matter what she did, however kinky and adventurous to hold his attention, she could feel him slipping away.

When she missed her period she was sure it was a fluke. Ash had been pretty clear about the fact that he was sterile. And though their relationship had never been about love, it was mutually exclusive, so for almost three years they had never so much as used a condom.

But then her breasts started to feel tender, and her appetite suddenly became insatiable. She knew even before she took the pregnancy test that it would be positive. And of course it was. Ash had made it clear on more than one occasion that he didn't want to be tied down. But he was a good man, and she knew he would do the right thing. The question was, did she want to be stuck in a relationship with a man who didn't want her or her child?

If she left Ash, she would have to quit law school, though honestly, she'd lost her interest in the law a while ago. She just hadn't had the heart to tell Ash. He had invested so much in her education. How could she tell him it was all for nothing?

She had been in the shower, debating her next move, when Ash came in with the video camera. She felt exhausted, and depressed, and in no mood to play the vixen, and really saw no point. She had already pretty much decided what she had to do. There was no need to keep trying to impress him. Three years of playing the role of the perfect woman had left her utterly exhausted. But when he stepped in the shower and started touching her, started kissing her, more tenderly than he ever had before, she melted. And when he made love to her, she could swear that for the first time he actually saw her. The *real* her. She let herself believe that somewhere deep down maybe he loved her.

For two weeks she agonized over what to do. She let herself hope that he would be happy about the baby. Then he came home from work in a foul mood, ranting about Jason Reagart being forced to marry and have a child he hadn't planned or expected. He said how lucky he was to have a woman who respected his boundaries. She knew then that her fantasy about her, Ash and the baby was never going to happen.

That was last night. Today she was leaving.

She stuffed the rest of her things in her case, leaving the cocktail dresses and sexy lingerie behind. She wouldn't be needing them where she was going. They wouldn't fit in a few months anyway. She zipped it up and hauled both pieces of luggage off the bed. Her entire life in two suitcases and an overstuffed duffel bag. She was twenty-four with hardly anything to show for it. But that was going to change. She was going to have a child to love, and maybe someday she might meet a man who appreciated her for who she really was.

She lugged the bags to the front door then grabbed her purse from the kitchen counter. She checked to make sure the six thousand was safely tucked inside. It was money she had been gradually accumulating over the past three years and saving for a rainy day.

When it rained it poured.

Next to the stack of credit cards Ash had given her, Mel set a notepad and pen out so she could write Ash a letter, but the truth was, she didn't have a clue what to say. She could thank him for all he'd done for her, but hadn't she thanked him enough already? She could tell him she was sorry, but honestly, she wasn't. She was giving him his freedom. Wasn't that enough?

She didn't doubt he would find someone to replace her, and in a few weeks she would be just a distant memory.

She grabbed her bags and opened the door, took one last look around, then left that life behind for good.

One

April

Asher Williams was not a patient man by nature. When he wanted something, he didn't like to wait, and truth be told, he rarely had to. However, he was warned, when he enlisted the services of a private investigator, that finding a missing person could take time. Particularly if the person they were looking for didn't want to be found. That being the case, he was surprised when he received a call from him a mere two days later.

Ash was in a meeting with several of his colleagues and wouldn't normally answer his cell phone, but when he saw the P.I.'s number on the screen, he made an exception. He suspected it was either very good news, or very bad.

"Excuse me for just a minute," he told his colleagues. He rose from his chair and walked across the room, out of earshot. "You have news?" he asked, then heard the three words he had been hoping for.

"I found her."

In that instant he felt a confusing and disturbing combination of relief and bitterness. "Where is she?"

"She's been staying in Abilene, Texas."

What the hell was she doing in *Texas?*

That wasn't important now. What mattered was bringing her back home where she belonged. And the only way to do that was to go and get her. He was sure, with some convincing, he could make her see that he knew what was best for her, that leaving him had been a mistake. "I'm in a meeting. I'll call you back in five minutes."

He hung up the phone and turned to his colleagues.

"Sorry, but I have to go," he told them. "And I'm not sure when I'll be back. Hopefully no more than a few days. I'll let you know when I have more details."

The look of stunned confusion on their faces as he walked from the room was mildly amusing, and not at all unexpected. In all his time as CFO of Maddox Communications, Ash had never missed a meeting or taken a sick day. He had never been so much as five minutes late for work, and he honestly couldn't recall the last time he'd taken a vacation—much less one with two minutes' notice.

On his way into his office Ash asked his secretary, Rachel, to hold all his calls. "And cancel any appointments I have for the next week, just to be safe."

Her eyes went wide. "A *week?*"

He closed his office door and settled behind his desk, his mind racing a million miles an hour with all that he needed to do before he left as he dialed the P.I.'s number. He answered on the first ring.

"You told me it could take months to find her," Ash said. "Are you sure you have the right Melody Trent?"

"I'm positive it's her. Your girlfriend was in an auto accident. It's how I found her so quickly."

Melody Trent wasn't his girlfriend. By definition, she was his mistress—a warm body to come home to after a long day at work. He paid her law school tuition and living expenses and she offered companionship with no strings attached. Just the way he liked it. But it was no time to split hairs.

"Was she injured?" he asked, expecting, at worst, a few bumps and bruises. He truly was not prepared for what the P.I. said next.

"According to the police report, the driver, your girl-friend, was pretty banged up and there was one fatality."

Ash's stomach bottomed out and his mouth went dry. "How banged up?"

"She's been in the hospital for a couple of weeks."

"You said there was a fatality. What happened exactly?" He rose from his chair, began pacing as the P.I. gave him what few details he had about the crash. And it was bad. Worse than Ash could have ever imagined. "Is Melody being held responsible?"

"Fortunately, no. The police filed it as an accident. That doesn't mean there won't be a civil suit, though."

They would deal with that when and if the time came. "How is Melody? Do you have any details on her condition?"

"All the hospital would say is that she's stable. They'll only give details to family. When I asked to talk to her, they said she wasn't taking phone calls. That usually means that for whatever reason, the patient is unable to speak. My best guess would be she's unconscious."

Since Melody left him, Ash had been counting the hours

until she came crawling back to ask forgiveness, to say that she'd made a mistake. At least now he knew why she hadn't. Although that wasn't much of a consolation. And he would be damned if anyone was going to stop him from learning the truth. "I guess I'll just have to be family."

"You going to say she's your long-lost sister or something?" the PI asked.

"Of course not." He needed something a bit more believable. Something he could easily prove.

Melody was his fiancée.

The next morning Ash caught the earliest flight to the Dallas/Fort Worth airport, then rented a car and made the two-and-a-half-hour drive to Abilene. He had called ahead the afternoon before, setting up a meeting with the doctor in charge of her care. They told him that Melody was conscious and out of the woods, but that was the most they would say over the phone.

Once he got to the hospital he strode right past the registration desk. He'd learned a long time ago that if he looked as though he belonged somewhere, showed he was in charge, people naturally followed along, and no one tried to stop him as he stepped onto the elevator. He got off on the third floor, surprised to realize that he was actually nervous. What if Melody didn't want to come back to him?

Of course she would, he assured himself. Her leaving had obviously been a great error in judgment, and it would have only been a matter of time before she realized how much she missed him. Besides, where else would she go while she healed from her injuries? She needed him.

He stopped at the nurses' station and they paged a Dr. Nelson. He appeared less than five minutes later.

"Mr. Williams?" he said, shaking Ash's hand. The

department on his name badge was neurology, which likely meant that Melody had suffered some sort of brain injury. Which explained why she would have been unconscious. But did it mean her injuries were even more serious than he could have imagined? What if she never made a full recovery?

"Where is my fiancée?" Ash asked, surprised by the note of panic in his voice. He needed to hold it together. Barging in and making demands would only make this more difficult. Especially if Melody told them he actually wasn't her fiancé. He took a second to collect himself and asked, in a much calmer tone, "Can I see her?"

"Of course, but why don't we have a talk first."

He wanted to see Melody now, but he followed the doctor to a small family waiting room by the elevator. The room was empty, but for a television in the corner playing some daytime game show. He sat and gestured for Ash to join him.

"How much do you know about the accident?" the doctor asked.

"I was told that the car rolled, and there was one fatality."

"Your fiancée is a very lucky woman, Mr. Williams. She was driving on a back road when the crash occurred and it was several hours before someone drove past and discovered her there. She was airlifted here for treatment, but if the local EMS team hadn't worked so quickly, you would be having this conversation with the coroner."

A knot twisted his insides. It was surreal to imagine that he had come so close to losing Melody for good, and the thought of her lying trapped and alone, not knowing if she would live or die, made him sick to his stomach. He may have been angry that she left him, but he still cared deeply for her. "What was the extent of her injuries?"

"She suffered a subdural hematoma."

"A brain injury?"

He nodded. "Until two days ago she's been in a drug-induced coma."

"But she'll recover?"

"We expect her to make a full recovery."

Ash's relief was so intense, his body went limp. If he hadn't already been sitting, he was sure his legs would have given out from under him.

"Although," the doctor added, his expression darkening, "there were a few…complications."

Ash frowned. "What complications?"

"I'm sorry to have to tell you that she lost the baby."

"Baby?" he asked, the doctor's words not making any sense. Melody wasn't having a baby.

The doctor blinked. "I'm sorry, I just assumed you knew that she was pregnant."

Why would Ash even suspect such a thing when the radiation from childhood cancer had rendered him sterile? It had to be a mistake. "You're *sure?*"

"Absolutely."

The only explanation, Ash realized, was that Melody had been cheating on him. The knot in his gut twisted tighter, making it difficult to take a full breath. Is that where Melody had been going when she left him? To be with her lover? The father of her child?

And like a love-sick fool Ash had been chasing after her, prepared to convince her to come home. She had betrayed him, after all that he had done for her, and he hadn't suspected a damned thing.

His first reaction was to get up, walk out of the hospital and never look back, but his body refused to cooperate. He needed to see her, just one last time. He needed to know why the hell she would do this to him, when he had given her everything she had ever asked for, everything she could have ever needed. She could have at least had the decency, and the courage, to be honest with him.

He could see that the doctor was curious to know why, as her fiancé, Ash hadn't known about the pregnancy, but Ash didn't feel he owed him or anyone else an explanation. "How far along was she?" he asked.

"Around fourteen weeks, we think."

"You think? Didn't she say?"

"We haven't mentioned the miscarriage. We think it would be too upsetting at this point in her recovery."

"So she believes she's still pregnant?"

"She has no idea that she was pregnant when she was in the accident."

Ash frowned. That made no sense. "How could she not know?"

"I'm sorry to have to tell you, Mr. Williams, but your fiancée has amnesia."

The gripping fingers of a relentless headache squeezed Melody's brain. A dull, insistent throb, as though a vice was being cranked tighter and tighter against her skull.

"Time for your pain meds," her nurse chirped, materializing at the side of the bed as though Melody had summoned her by sheer will.

Or had she hit the call button? She honestly couldn't remember. Things were still a bit fuzzy, but the doctor told her that was perfectly normal. She just needed time for the anesthesia to leave her system.

The nurse held out a small plastic cup of pills and a glass of water. "Can you swallow these for me, hon?"

Yes, she could, she thought, swallowing gingerly, the cool water feeling good on her scratchy throat. She knew how to swallow pills, and brush her teeth, and control the television remote. She could use a fork and a knife and she'd had no trouble reading the gossip rags the nurse had brought for her.

So why, she wondered, did she not recognize her own name?

She couldn't recall a single thing about her life, not even the auto accident that was apparently responsible for her current condition. As for her life before the accident, it was as if someone had reached inside her head and wiped her memory slate clean.

Post-traumatic amnesia, the neurologist called it, and when she'd asked how long it would last, his answer hadn't been encouraging.

"The brain is a mysterious organ. One we still know so little about," he'd told her. "Your condition could last a week, or a month. Or there's a possibility that it could be permanent. We'll just have to wait and see."

She didn't want to wait. She wanted answers *now*. Everyone kept telling her how lucky she'd been. Other than the head injury, she had escaped the accident relatively unscathed. A few bumps and bruises mostly. No broken bones or serious lacerations. No permanent physical scars. However, as she flipped through the television channels, knowing she must have favorite programs but seeing only unfamiliar faces, or as she picked at the food on her meal tray, clueless as to her likes and dislikes, she didn't feel very lucky. In fact, she felt cursed. As though God was punishing her for some horrible thing that she couldn't even remember doing.

The nurse checked her IV, jotted something on her chart, then told Melody, "Just buzz if you need anything."

Answers, Melody thought as the nurse disappeared into the hall. All she wanted was answers.

She reached up and felt the inch-long row of stitches

above her left ear where they had drilled a nickel-size hole to reduce the swelling on her brain, relieving the pressure that would have otherwise squeezed her damaged brain literally to death.

They had snatched her back from the brink of death, only now she wondered what kind of life they had snatched her back to. According to the social worker who had been in to see her, Melody had no living relatives. No siblings, no children, and no record of ever having been married. If she had friends or colleagues, she had no memory of them, and not a single person had come to visit her.

Had she always been this...alone?

Her address was listed as San Francisco, California— wherever that was—some sixteen hundred miles from the site of the accident. It perplexed her how she could still recognize words and numbers, while photos of the city she had supposedly lived in for three years drew a complete blank. She was also curious to know what she had been doing so far from home. A vacation maybe? Was she visiting friends? If so, wouldn't they have been concerned when she never showed up?

Or was it something more sinister?

After waking from the coma, she'd dumped the contents of her purse on the bed, hoping something might spark a memory. She was stunned when, along with a wallet, nail file, hairbrush and a few tubes of lip gloss, a stack of cash an inch thick tumbled out from under the bottom lining. She quickly shoved it back in the bag before anyone could see, and later that night, when the halls had gone quiet, she counted it. There had been over four thousand dollars in various denominations.

Was she on the run? Had she done something illegal? Maybe knocked off a convenience station on the way out of town? If so, wouldn't the police have arrested her by now?

She was sure there was some perfectly logical explanation. But just in case, for now anyway, she was keeping her discovery to herself. She kept the bag in bed with her at all times, the strap looped firmly around her wrist.

Just in case.

Melody heard voices in the hallway outside her room and craned her neck to see who was there. Two men stood just outside her door. Dr. Nelson, her neurologist, and a second man she didn't recognize. Which wasn't unusual seeing as how she didn't recognize anyone.

Could he be another doctor maybe? God knew she had seen her share in the past couple of days. But something about him, the way he carried himself, even though she only saw him in profile, told her he wasn't a part of the hospital staff. This man was someone…important. Someone of a higher authority.

The first thing that came to mind of course was a police detective, and her heart did a somersault with a triple twist. Maybe the police had seen the money in her purse and they sent someone to question her. Then she realized that no one on a public servant's pay could afford such an expensive suit. She didn't even know how she knew that it was expensive, but she did. Somewhere deep down she instinctively knew she should recognize the clothes designer, yet the name refused to surface. And it didn't escape her attention how well the man inside the suit wore it. She didn't doubt it was tailored to fit him exclusively.

The man listened intently as the doctor spoke, nodding occasionally. Who could he be? Did he know her? He must, or why else would they be standing in her doorway?

The man turned in her direction, caught her blatantly staring, and when his eyes met hers, her heart did that weird flippy thing again. The only way to describe him was…intense. His eyes were clear and intelligent, his build long and lean, his features sharp and angular. And he was ridiculously attractive. Like someone straight off the television or the pages of her gossip mags.

He said a few words to the doctor, his eyes never straying from hers, then entered her room, walking to the bed, no hesitation or reserve, that air of authority preceding him like a living, breathing entity.

Whoever this man was, he knew exactly what he wanted, and she didn't doubt he would go to any lengths to get it.

"You have a visitor, Melody." Only when Dr. Nelson spoke did she realize he'd walked in, too.

The man stood silently beside her bed, watching her with eyes that were a striking combination of green and brown flecks rimmed in deep amber—as unique and intense as the rest of him.

He looked as though he expected her to say something. She wasn't sure what though.

Dr. Nelson walked around to stand at the opposite side of her bed, his presence a comfort as she felt herself begin to wither under the stranger's scrutiny. Why did he look at her that way? Almost as though he was angry with her.

"Does he look familiar to you?" Dr. Nelson asked.

He was undeniably easy on the eyes, but she couldn't say that she'd ever seen him before. Melody shook her head. "Should he?"

The men exchanged a look, and for some reason her heart sank.

"Melody," Dr. Nelson said, in a soothing and patient voice. "This Asher Williams. Your fiancé."

Two

Melody shook her head, unwilling to accept what the doctor was telling her. She didn't even know why. It just didn't feel right. Maybe it was the way he was looking at her, as if her being in an accident had somehow been a slight against him. Shouldn't he be relieved that she was alive?

So where were his tears of joy? Why didn't he gather her up and hold her?

"No, he isn't," she said.

The doctor frowned, and her so-called fiancé looked taken aback.

"You remember?" Dr. Nelson asked.

"No. But I just know. That man can't be my fiancé."

Tension hung like a foul odor in the room. No one seemed to know what to do or say next.

"Would you excuse us, Doctor?" her imposter fiancé said, and Melody felt a quick and sharp stab of panic. She didn't want to be alone with him. Something about his presence was just so disconcerting.

"I'd like him to stay," she said.

"Actually, I do have patients I need to see." He flashed Melody an encouraging smile and gave her arm a gentle pat. "The nurse is just down the hall if you need anything."

That wasn't very reassuring. What did they even know about this man? Did they check out his story at all, or take him on his word? He could be a rapist or an ax murderer. A criminal who preyed on innocent women with amnesia. Or even worse, maybe he was the person she had taken that cash from. Maybe he was here for revenge.

She tucked her purse closer to her side under the covers, until she was practically sitting on it.

The phrase *never show fear* popped into her head, although from where, she didn't have a clue. But it was smart advice, so she lifted her chin as he grabbed a chair and pulled it up to the side of her bed. He removed his jacket and draped it over the back before he sat down. He wasn't a big man, more lean than muscular, so why did she feel this nervous energy? This instinct to run?

He eased the chair closer to her side and she instinctively jerked upright. So much for not showing fear. Even in repose the man had an assuming presence.

"You don't have to be afraid of me," he said.

"Do you honestly expect me to just take your word that we're engaged?" she asked. "You could be…*anyone*."

"Do you have your driver's license?"

"Why?"

He reached into his back pants pocket and she tensed again. "Relax. I'm just grabbing my wallet. Look at the address on my driver's license." He handed his wallet to her.

The first thing she noticed, as she flipped it open, was

that there were no photos, nothing of a personal nature, and the second thing was the thick stack of cash tucked inside. And yes, the address on his license was the same as hers. She knew without checking her own license because she had read it over and over about a thousand times yesterday, hoping it would trigger some sort of memory. A visual representation of the place she'd lived.

Of course, it hadn't.

She handed his wallet back to him, and he stuck it in his pocket. "That doesn't prove anything. If we're really engaged, where is my ring?" She held up her hand, so he could see her naked finger. A man of his obvious wealth would have bought the woman he planned to marry a huge rock.

He reached into his shirt pocket and produced a ring box. He snapped it open and inside was a diamond ring with a stone so enormous and sparkly it nearly took her breath away. "One of the prongs came loose and it was at the jeweler's being repaired."

He handed it to her, but she shook her head. She still wasn't ready to accept this. Although, what man would offer what must have been a ridiculously expensive ring to a woman who wasn't his fiancée?

Of course, one quick thwack with the ax and it would easily be his again.

She cringed and chastised herself for the gruesome thought.

"Maybe you should hang on to it for now, just to be safe," she told him.

"No. I don't care if you believe me or not." He rose from his chair and reached for her hand, and it took everything in her not to flinch. "This belongs to you."

The ring slid with ease on her finger. A perfect fit. Could

it just be a coincidence? It was becoming increasingly difficult not to believe him.

"I have these, too," he said, leaning down to take a stack of photos from the inside of his jacket. He gave them to her, then sat back down.

The pictures were indeed of her and this Asher person. She skimmed them, and in each and every one they were either smiling or laughing or…*oh, my*…some were rather racy in nature.

Her cheeks blushed brightly and a grin quirked up the corner of his mouth. "I included a few from our *personal* collection, so there wouldn't be any doubt."

In one of the shots Asher wore nothing but a pair of boxer briefs and the sight of all that lean muscle and smooth skin caused an unexpected jab of longing that she felt deep inside her belly. A memory, maybe, or just a natural female reaction to the sight of an attractive man.

"I have video, as well," he said. She was going to ask what kind of video, but his expression said it all. The look in his eyes was so steamy it nearly melted her. "Due to their scandalous nature, I felt it best to leave them at home," he added.

Melody couldn't imagine she was the type of woman who would let herself be photographed, or even worse videotaped, in a compromising position with a man she didn't trust completely.

Maybe Asher Williams really was her fiancé.

Ash's first suspicion, when the doctor told him Melody had amnesia, was that she was faking it. But then he asked himself, why would she? What logical reason did she have to pretend that she didn't know him? Besides, he doubted that anyone in her physical condition could convincingly fabricate the look of bewildered shock she wore when the doctor told her Ash was her fiancé.

Of course, she had managed to keep the baby she was carrying a secret, and the affair she'd been having. After the initial shock of her betrayal had worn off, he'd felt nothing but seething, bone-deep anger. After all he had done for her—paying her living expenses and college tuition, giving her credit cards to purchase everything her greedy heart had desired, taking care of her for *three* years—how could she so callously betray him?

Coincidentally, just like his ex-wife. He hadn't had a clue then either. One would think he'd have learned his lesson the first time. And though his first instinct had been to walk out the door and never look back, he'd had an even better idea.

This time he would get revenge.

He would keep up the ruse of their engagement and take Melody home. He would make her fall in love with him, depend on him, then he would betray her, just as coldheartedly and callously as she had him. And he wouldn't lose a single night's sleep over it.

"What was I doing in Texas alone?" Melody asked him, still not totally convinced.

Ash had anticipated this question and had an answer already prepared. "A research trip."

"Research for what?"

"A paper you were working on for school."

She looked puzzled. "I go to school?"

"You're in law school."

"I am?" she asked, looking stunned.

"You have a year to go before you take the bar exam."

Her brow furrowed and she reached up to rub her temple. "Not if I can't remember anything I've learned."

"I don't care what the doctors say," he told her, taking her hand, and this time she didn't flinch. "You'll get your memory back."

Her grateful smile almost filled him with guilt. Almost.

"So you just let me go on this trip, no questions asked?"

He gave her hand a squeeze. "I trust you, Mel."

The comment hit its mark, and the really pathetic thing was that it used to be true. He never would have guessed that Melody would do something like this to him.

"How long was I gone?"

"A few weeks," he lied. "I began to worry when you stopped answering your phone. I tried to find you myself, but that went nowhere fast. I was beside myself with worry, Mel. I thought something terrible had happened. I thought...I thought that you were dead. That I would never see you again." The fabricated emotion in his voice sounded genuine, even to his own ears, and Melody was eating it up. "The police were no help, so I hired a private detective."

"And here you are."

He nodded. "Here I am. And I would really like to hold my fiancée. If she would let me."

Melody bit her lip, and with gratitude in her eyes, held her arms out. She bought his bull—hook, line and sinker. This was almost too easy.

Ash rose from his chair and sat on the edge of her bed, and when he took her in his arms and she melted against him, soft and warm and a little fragile, he had a flash of something that felt like relief, or maybe satisfaction, then he reminded himself exactly what it was that brought them to this place. How deeply she had betrayed him. His first instinct was to push her away, but he had to play the role of the loving fiancé.

She let her head rest on his shoulder and her arms slipped around his back. The contour of her body felt so familiar to him, and he couldn't help wondering what it must have been like for her, holding a stranger. Some deep place inside him wanted to feel sympathy, but she had brought this on herself. If she hadn't cheated on him, hadn't stolen away like a criminal, she never would have been in the accident and everything would be normal.

As her arms tightened around him, he did notice that she felt frailer than before, as though not only had she lost pounds, but muscle mass. Their building had an exercise room and as long as Ash had known her, Melody had been almost fanatical about staying in shape. He wondered if this would be a blow to her ego.

But how could it be if she didn't even remember she *had* an ego? Or maybe that was something that was inborn.

Under the circumstances Ash didn't expect the embrace to last long, and he kept waiting for her to pull away. Instead she moved closer, held him tighter, and after a moment he realized that she was trembling.

"Are you okay?" he asked, lifting a hand to stroke her hair.

"I'm scared," she said, her voice small and soft. Melody wasn't a crier—in three years together he could recall only two times he'd even seen the sheen of moisture in her eyes—but he could swear that now he heard tears in her voice.

"What are you scared of?" he asked, stroking her hair and her back, pretending to comfort her, when in reality he felt that she was getting exactly what she deserved.

"Everything," she said. "I'm afraid of all I don't know,

and everything I need to learn. What if I'm never..." She shook her head against his chest.

He held her away from him, so he could see her face. Melody was a fighter. Much like himself, when she wanted something, she went after it with all pistons firing. It was what had drawn him to her in the first place. But right now, he couldn't recall ever seeing her look more pale and distraught, and he actually had to harden his heart to keep from feeling sorry for her.

She had brought this on herself.

"If you never what?" he asked.

Her eyes were full of uncertainty. "What if I can't be the person I was before? What if the accident changed me? What will I do with my life? Who will I be?"

Not the heartless betrayer she had been before the accident. Not if he had anything to do with it. He would break her spirit, so no other man would have to suffer the same humiliation he had.

A tear spilled over onto her cheek and he wiped it away with his thumb, cradling her cheek in his palm. "Why don't you concentrate on getting better? Everything will work out. I promise."

Looking as though she desperately wanted to believe him, she leaned her head back down and sighed against his shoulder. And maybe she did believe him, because she was no longer shaking.

"I'm getting sleepy," she said.

"I'm not surprised. You've had an eventful morning. Why don't you lie down?"

He helped her lie back against the pillows. She did look exhausted. Mentally and physically.

He pulled the covers up and tucked them around her, much the way his mother had for him when he was a boy. When he'd been sick, and weakened by the radiation, she'd somehow managed to be there every evening to kiss him goodnight, despite working two, and sometimes three jobs at a time to keep their heads above water. Until she'd literally worked herself to death.

Though Ash was declared cancer free by his thirteenth birthday, the medical bills had mounted. His father had been too lazy and most times too drunk to hold down a job, so the responsibility of taking care of them had fallen solely on his mother. And due to their debt, annual trips to the doctor for preventative care that wasn't covered by their insurance had been a luxury she couldn't afford. By the time she'd begun getting symptoms and the cancer was discovered, it had already metastasized and spread to most of her major organs. The news had sent his father into a downward spiral, and it was left up to Ash to take care of her.

Eight months later, and barely a week after Ash graduated from high school, she was gone. For years, he felt partially responsible for her death. Had it not been for his own cancer, they might have caught hers sooner, when it was still treatable.

The day of his mother's funeral was the day Ash had written his father out of his life for good. His aunt had contacted him several years later to let him know that his father had passed away. Advanced liver cirrhosis. Ash didn't go to the funeral.

By then Ash was living in California, and going to school. Like his mother, he worked two and three jobs to make ends meet. Despite that, he'd somehow managed to maintain a near-perfect GPA. After graduation he'd married his college sweetheart and landed a job with Maddox Communications, convinced he was living the American dream. Unfortunately things had not been what they seemed.

The day he was offered the position of CFO, what should have been one of the best days of his life, he'd learned that his wife was having an affair. She'd claimed she did it because she was lonely. He'd worked such long hours he was never there for her. She sure hadn't minded spending the money he earned working those long hours, though. Not to mention, when he *had* been home, the "I have a headache" excuse was a regular. The irony of it would have been laughable had he not been so completely devastated.

Granted, theirs had never been a particularly passionate marriage, but he'd thought they were relatively happy. Apparently not. And the worst part had been that he hadn't suspected a thing.

Ash had thought he was through with women for good, but only a few months after the divorce was final he met Melody. She was young and beautiful and bright, and he was fascinated by her spunk and enthusiasm. Probably because he saw much of himself mirrored back in her eyes.

They had come from similar humble beginnings, and, like him, she was determined to succeed. They'd started dating in early April. The last week of May when the sublet on her apartment expired, he'd suggested she stay with him until she found another place, and she just never left.

Since then they seemed to have an unwritten understanding. She made herself accessible to him in any capacity necessary with no strings attached. There were no sentiments of love or talk of marriage, no questions or accusations when he worked late or cancelled a date. In return he provided financial security.

At times, he couldn't help thinking he was getting the better end of the deal. Not only did he have a willing mistress at his disposal 24/7, he also had the satisfaction of knowing that he was helping her make something of her life. If his mother had someone like that, someone to take care of her, she might still be alive.

Helping Melody had, in his own way, been a tribute to his mother. An homage to her strength and character, and as far as he was concerned, Melody had betrayed her, too.

He gazed down at Melody and realized she was sound asleep. For several minutes he just watched her, wondering what could have driven her to be unfaithful to him. When had she changed her mind, and decided that she wanted more than what they had? And why hadn't she just told him the truth? If she'd truly wanted out, he would have respected that. He wouldn't have liked it, and he would have tried to talk her out of leaving, but he would have eventually let her go. No strings attached.

Instead she had thrown back in his face everything he had ever done for her.

"How is she?" someone asked, and Ash turned to see Dr. Nelson standing in the doorway.

"Sleeping."

"I just wanted to stop back in once more before I left."

"I'm glad you did. We never discussed when I could take her home. I'd like to make travel arrangements."

He gestured Ash into the hall. "If she continues to improve, I would say a week to ten days."

"That long? She seems to be doing so well."

"She suffered a severe brain injury. You can't necessarily see the damage, but believe me, it's there." He paused then added, "When you say home, I assume you mean California."

"Of course."

"You should know that flying will be out of the question."

"Not even in my company's private jet?"

"She had a brain bleed. The change in pressure could very literally kill her. Frankly, I'm not crazy about the idea of her being on the road for that long either, but I guess there aren't any other options."

Sixteen hundred miles trapped in a car together. Not his idea of fun. Besides, he wanted to get her home and settled before she remembered something. If she ever did.

"I was wondering," Ash said. "If she does regain her memory, how long will it take?"

"There's no definitive answer that I can give you, Mr. Williams. If she does regain any memories, it can be a slow and sometimes traumatic process. Just be thankful that she's doing as well as she is. It will just take time and patience."

Unfortunately he had little of either.

"Even if she doesn't regain her memories," he added, "there's no reason to expect that you two won't live a long and happy life together regardless."

Actually, there was one damned good reason. Whether she remembered it or not, Melody had crossed him. It was time she got a taste of her own medicine.

But to make this work, Ash had a bit of cleaning up to do first.

Three

When Melody opened her eyes again, Ash wasn't in the room. She had the sudden, terrifying sensation that everything that had happened earlier was a dream or a hallucination. Then she lifted her hand, saw the diamond on her ring finger and relief washed over her.

It was real.

But where did Ash go? She pushed herself up on her elbows to look around and saw the note he'd left on the tray beside her:

> Went to get your things. Back later to see you.
> XOXO
> Ash

She wondered where he was going to get them, then realized she must have been staying in a hotel when she'd had her accident. But that was more than two weeks ago.

Wouldn't they have discarded her things by now? Did hotels hang on to the items abandoned by their customers?

She hoped so. Maybe there was something among her things that would spark a memory, and she was interested to see this so-called research Ash had been talking about. Not that she didn't believe him. It was just that something about this whole scenario was...off.

If what he said was true, and she was only here for school, what was she doing with four thousand dollars hidden in the lining of her purse? Was she trying to bribe someone, or buy information? Had she gotten herself into something illegal that she had been afraid to tell him? What if her accident hadn't been an accident after all?

And even worse, what if the person she was trying to get away from was Ash?

She realized just how ridiculous that sounded and that she was letting her imagination run away from her. She'd seen the photos; they were obviously very happy together. She was sure that the expression she'd mistaken for anger when he'd first entered her room was just his reaction to learning that she didn't remember him. After all, how would she feel if the man she had planned to spend the rest of her life with forgot who she was? Then insisted that she supply proof of their relationship? That would be devastating.

There were other things that disturbed her, as well. It seemed as though the news that she was in law school would evoke some sort of emotion. If not excitement, then maybe mild curiosity. Instead she'd just felt...disconnected. As though he were talking about another woman's life. One she had little interest in. And in a way maybe she was.

She was sure that once she got home and back into a regular routine, things would come back to her. She would be more interested in things like her career and her hobbies. If she had any hobbies. She hadn't even thought to ask him. There were all sorts of things he could tell her about her life.

She heard footsteps in the hall, her spirits lifting when she thought it might be Ash, but it was only the nurse.

"I see you're awake," she said with her usual cheery disposition. "How are you feeling?"

"Better," she said, and it was true. She still had a million questions, but at least now she knew that when she was discharged from the hospital, she would have somewhere to go. There was someone out there who loved and cared about her.

"I saw your fiancé," the nurse said as she checked Melody's IV. "He's very handsome. But that just stands to reason, I guess."

"Why?"

"Well, because you're so pretty."

"I am?"

The nurse laughed. "Well, of course you are."

She made it sound so obvious, but when Melody had seen her reflection the other day, the only thing she noticed was that a stranger's eyes stared back at her. She didn't stop to consider whether she was attractive. It just didn't seem important at the time.

"I hear that you're in law school," the nurse said, jotting something down on Melody's chart. "I never would have guessed."

"Why is that?"

She shrugged. "Oh, I don't know. I guess you just don't seem the type. I think of lawyers as pushy and overbearing. You're not like that at all."

She wondered what she *was* like, but she was a little afraid to ask.

The nurse closed her chart and asked, "Is there anything you need?"

She shook her head.

"Okay, well, you ring if you need me."

When she was gone Melody considered what she said. What if she really wasn't cut out to be a lawyer? Would she be throwing all those years of school down the toilet?

But honestly, what did the nurse know of her? She was not going to plan the rest of her life around a comment made by someone who had known her for less than three days. And not at her best, obviously. Maybe when she was back on her feet and feeling like her old self she would be lawyer material again. A real shark.

Or, as she had considered earlier, maybe the accident had changed her.

There was really no point in worrying about it now. Like the doctor said, she needed to concentrate on healing. It was sage advice, because the sooner she got back to her life, the sooner she would get her memory back. And in the meantime she was sure, with a fiancé like Ash to take care of her, everything was going to be okay.

Ash stood in the impound lot at the Abilene police station, heart in the pit of his stomach, knees weak, looking at what was left of Melody's Audi Roadster. Suddenly he understood why everyone kept saying that she was lucky to be alive.

Not only was it totaled, it was barely recognizable. He knew it was a rollover accident, he just hadn't realized how *far* it had rolled, and the momentum it had gained by the time it hit the tree that had ultimately stopped it. The passenger's side was pretty much gone, completely crushed inward.

Had she hit the tree on the driver's side, there was no

doubt she wouldn't have survived. Also, Mel always drove with the top down, but apparently it had been raining, so when she flipped over there was at least something there to keep her from snapping her neck. Although just barely, because the top, too, was crushed, and at some point had come loose and was hanging by a single bolt.

He hated Melody for what she had done to him, but he wouldn't wish an accident like this on his worst enemy.

According to the police, she'd tried to swerve out of the way when she saw the bike. Unfortunately it had been too late.

He walked over and peered in the driver's side, immediately seeing what he was looking for. He tried the door but it was hopelessly jammed. With one hand he pushed the top out of the way then reached around the steering wheel and grabbed the keys from the ignition. He hit the release for the trunk, but it didn't budge, and he had no better luck with the key. If there was anything in there, she was going to have to live without it.

He turned to walk back to the entrance, then as an afterthought, walked back and snapped some pictures with his phone. The matter had already been reported to his insurance company, but it never hurt to be thorough and keep a record for his own reference.

When he was back in his rental car, he punched the address the P.I. had given him into the GPS and followed the commands until he was parked in front of a house about fifteen minutes from the hospital.

The house itself was tiny but well-kept, although the neighborhood left a lot to be desired. How could she go from a penthouse condo to living in what was barely a step above a slum? To be with her lover? If so, the guy had to be a loser. Although if she had come here to be with her lover, why hadn't he been at the hospital with her?

Well, if there was someone else there, he was about to find out.

There were no cars in the driveway, and the curtains were drawn. He walked to the front door with purpose, slid the key in, and opened it. The first thing that hit him was a rush of cool air punctuated by the rancid stench of rotting food. At that point he knew it was safe to assume that she lived alone. No one would be able to stand the odor.

Covering his face with a handkerchief, he walked through a small living room with outdated, discount-store furniture, snapping on lights and opening windows as he made to the kitchen. He saw the culprit right away, an unopened package of ground beef on a faded, worn countertop, next to a stove that was probably older than him. She must have taken it out to thaw right before the accident.

He opened the kitchen window, then, for the landlord's sake he grabbed the package and tossed it in the freezer. He was sure the contents of the fridge were similarly frightening, but since neither he nor Mel would be returning, he didn't feel compelled to check.

There was nothing else remarkable about the room, so he moved on to explore the rest of the house.

The bathroom counter was covered with various toiletries that he didn't recognize—and why would he when they didn't share a bathroom—but everything was distinctly feminine. He checked the medicine chest and the cabinet below the sink but there was no evidence that a man had ever lived there.

He searched her bedroom next, finding more old and tacky furniture, and an unmade bed. Which was odd because back home she always kept things tidy and spotless. He found a lot of familiar-looking clothes in the closet and drawers, but again, nothing to suggest she'd had any male companionship. Not even a box of condoms in the bedside table. He and Melody had at one time kept them handy, but not for quite some time. They were monogamous, and he was sterile, so there really never seemed a point.

She had obviously had unprotected sex with someone, or she wouldn't have gotten pregnant. It hadn't even occurred to him earlier, but now he wondered if he should go get himself tested for STDs. Melody had callously put her own health and his in jeopardy. One more thing to hold against her.

He searched the entire room, top to bottom, but didn't find the one thing he was looking for. He was about to leave when, as an afterthought, Ash pulled back the comforter on the bed and hit pay dirt.

Melody's computer.

In the past he would have never betrayed her trust by looking through her computer. He respected her privacy, just as she respected his. But she had lost that particular privilege when she betrayed him. Besides, the information it contained might be the only clue as to who she was sleeping with. The only explanation as to why she left him. She owed him that much.

He wanted to look at it immediately but he honestly wasn't sure how much longer he could stand the stench and he still had to pack Melody's things. Most of her clothes he would ship home and have his secretary put away, keeping only a smaller bag in Texas, to make his two-week trip story more believable.

He looked at his watch and realized he was going to have to get moving if he was going to get back to the hospital before visiting hours were over. Though he was exhausted, and wanted nothing more that to go back to the hotel and take a hot shower, he had to play the role of the doting fiancé.

He crammed her things into the suitcases he found stored in her bedroom closet, shoved everything into the trunk of his rental car to sort later, then headed back to the hospital, but when he got there she was sleeping. Realizing that he hadn't eaten since that morning—and then only a hurried fast-food sandwich before his flight boarded—rather than eat an overpriced, sub-par meal in the cafeteria, he found a family diner a few blocks away. It wasn't the Ritz, but the food was decent, and he had the sneaking suspicion he would be eating there a lot in the next week to ten days. When he got back to Mel's room she was awake, sitting up and clearly relieved and excited to see him. "I was afraid you wouldn't make it back."

"I said in my note that I would be back. I just had a few things to take care of." He pulled up a chair but she patted the bed for him to sit beside her.

She looked a lot better than she had earlier. Her eyes were brighter and there was more color in her cheeks, and as he sat, he noticed that her hair was damp. As if reading his mind, she said, "They let me take a shower. It felt *so* wonderful. And tomorrow they want me to start walking, to get the strength back in my legs."

"That's good, right?"

"The nurse said the sooner I'm up and moving around on my own, the sooner they'll discharge me." She reached for his hand, and he had no choice but to take it. "I can hardly wait to go home. I'm sure that once I'm there, I'll start to remember things."

He hoped not. At least, not for a while. That could definitely complicate things. "I'm sure it will," he told her.

"Did the hotel still have my things?" she asked hopefully.

"Hotel?"

Her brow furrowed. "I just assumed I was staying at a hotel, while I did my research."

He cursed himself for letting his guard down. The last thing he wanted was to rouse her suspicions. He swiftly backpedaled.

"You were. I just thought for a second that you remembered something. And yes, they did. Your suitcase is in the trunk of my car. I'll keep it at my hotel until you're released."

"What about my research? Were there papers or files or anything?"

"Not that I saw," he said, realizing that the lies were coming easier now. "But your laptop was there."

Her eyes lit with excitement. "There might be something on it that will shake my memory!"

"I thought of that. I booted it up, but it's password protected, so unless you remember the password...." He watched as Melody's excitement fizzled away. "Tell you what," he said. "When we get back to San Francisco I'll have the tech people at work take a look at it. Maybe they can hack their way in."

"Okay," she agreed, looking a little less defeated, but he could see that she was disappointed.

In reality, he would be calling work at his soonest convenience and with any luck one of the tech guys could walk him through hacking the system himself. Only after he removed anything pertaining to the baby or the affair, or anything personal that might jog her memory, would he let her have it back.

It would be easier to have the hard drive reformatted, but that might look too suspicious. He'd thought of not mentioning the laptop at all, but it stood to reason that since she was a student, she would have one.

He could have lied and said it was destroyed in the accident, but unfortunately it was too late for that now.

"Can you do me a favor?" she asked.

"Sure."

"Can you tell me about myself?"

"Like what?"

"My family, my friends, where I'm from. Anything."

The truth was, despite living together for three years, he didn't know a heck of a lot about Melody. If she had friends at school, she didn't mention them, and when she wasn't in school, he really wasn't sure what she did with her time, other than cooking his dinners, cleaning their condo and of course shopping. She had always kept personal things pretty close to the vest. Either that or he had just never thought to ask.

But she looked so hopeful, he had to come up with something.

"Your mom died before I met you," he told her. "Ovarian cancer, I think. You told me that you never knew your real father, but you'd had something like five or six stepfathers growing up."

"Wow, that's a lot. Where did I grow up?"

He struggled to remember what she had told him when they first met. "All over, I think. You said that she moved you around a lot. I know you resented it."

Just as he had resented so many things from his own childhood. The cancer not even being the worst of it. But he was in no mood to dredge that up. Besides, she had no idea that he'd been sick. It just never came up. He and Mel knew each other, especially in the biblical sense, but they didn't really *know* each other.

He'd been so sure that was the way he'd wanted it, so jaded by his marriage, he never considered that he might want more. Not until it was too late.

Four

Melody had this look, like the playground bully had just stolen her candy. "Wow. It sounds like I had a pretty lousy childhood."

Ash felt a jab of guilt for painting such a grim picture.

"I'm sure there were good things," he told her. "You just never talked about it much."

"How did we meet?"

The memory brought a smile to his face. Now, this was something he remembered. "A company party. At Maddox Communications."

"That's where you work, right?"

He nodded. "You were there with some cocky junior rep. Brent somebody. A real jerk. But the instant I saw you standing by the bar, wearing this slinky little black number, I couldn't look away. Hell, every man in the room had their eye on you. He was droning on, probably thinking he was hot shit because he was with the sexiest woman at the party, and you had this look like you were counting the minutes until you could send him and his overinflated ego packing. You looked over and saw me watching you. You gave me a thorough once-over, then flashed me this sexy smile."

Her eyes went wide. "*I* did that?"

Her surprise made him laugh. "Yeah. At that point I had no choice but to rescue you. So I walked over and asked you to dance."

"How did my date feel about that?"

Ash grinned, recalling the shocked look on the kid's face, the indignant glare as Ash led Mel onto the dance floor and pulled her into his arms. "He didn't look very happy."

"What did he do?"

"What could he do? I was CFO, he was a lowly junior rep. I could have squashed him. Although, if memory serves, someone else eventually did. I don't think he lasted long with the firm."

"So we danced?" she said, a dreamy look on her face.

"All night." Ash had been the envy of every man at the party. At the time he'd still been reeling from his divorce and the ego boost was a welcome one. It wasn't until later that he realized just how thorough of a *boost* she intended to give him.

"Then what happened?" she asked.

"You asked if you could see my office, so I took you there. The instant the door closed we were all over each other."

She swallowed hard, looking as scandalized as she was intrigued. And maybe a little turned on, too. "Then what?"

"You really have to ask?"

"We had *sex* in your office?" she asked in a hushed voice, as if she worried someone would overhear. "Right after we met?"

This from the woman who had never hesitated to tell him exactly what she wanted, when she wanted it, in the bluntest of sexual terms. Language that would make a lot of women blush. Or blanch.

He grinned and nodded. "On the desk, on the sofa, in my chair. Up against the plate-glass window overlooking the bay."

Her cheeks flushed bright pink. "We did it against a *window?*"

"You've always had voyeuristic tendencies." He'd never met a woman more confident, more comfortable in her own skin, than Melody. Though he would never admit it aloud, her brazen nature could be the slightest bit intimidating at times.

But obviously now something had changed. There was a vulnerability in her eyes that he'd never seen before. A hesitance she had never shown. Truth be told, he kind of liked it. And maybe it softened him up just a little. He may have supported Mel for the past three years, but he would never make the mistake of thinking that she depended on him. Had she not met him, she would have managed just fine on her own.

He'd forgotten what it felt like to have someone need him.

"I can't believe I slept with you on the first date," she said. "I can't imagine what you must have thought of me."

"Actually, with my divorce barely final, it was exactly what I needed."

"You were married before?"

"For seven years."

"Why did you split up?"

"I guess you could say it was due to a total lack of appreciation."

"What do you mean?"

"She didn't appreciate the hours I worked, and I didn't appreciate her screwing her personal trainer in my bed."

She sucked in a surprised breath, clearly outraged on his behalf. "She *cheated* on you?"

"For quite some time as I understand it." He wondered how Melody would feel if she knew she had done the same thing? Although, as far as he knew, never in *his* bed. But that was just geography. Cheating was cheating.

Melody tightened her grip on his hand. He hadn't even realized she was holding it. It occurred to him suddenly how cozy this little scenario had become. Too cozy for his liking.

He pulled his hand free and looked at his watch. "It's late. I should let you get some sleep."

"Did I say something wrong?" she asked, looking troubled. "Because if it bothers you to talk about your ex, we can talk about something else."

Frankly, he was all talked out. He wasn't sure what else to say to her. And he wished she would stop being so… nice. Not that she hadn't been nice before, but she'd always had an edge. A sharp wit and a razor-edged tongue. Now she was being so sweet and understanding, she was making it tough for him to hold on to his anger. To be objective.

"You didn't say anything wrong. It's just, well, it's been a really long day. Maybe I'm the one who's tired."

"I'm sorry, I'm being selfish," she said, looking truly apologetic. "I didn't even take into consideration how hard this has been for you."

"It has been a long couple of weeks not knowing where

you were," he said, which only made her look more guilty. "I'm sure I'll feel better after a good night's sleep."

"Go," she said, making a shooing gesture. "Get some sleep."

"Are you sure? I can stay longer if you want me to."

"No. I'm tired anyway. I'll probably watch a few minutes of television then fall asleep."

He had the distinct feeling she was lying, because honestly, she didn't look the least bit tired. But he wasn't going to argue.

"I'll be back first thing tomorrow," he assured her, rising from the edge of the bed.

"Thank you," she said, her expression earnest.

"For what?"

"Telling me those things about myself. It makes me feel a little less…lost. Even if it wasn't quite what I expected."

"You're welcome," he said, and leaned down to brush a kiss across her forehead. "I'll see you tomorrow."

As he walked from the room he heard the television click on. He couldn't help feeling the slightest bit guilty for leaving her alone, but he had a charade to plan.

It turned out that Ash didn't need the help of the tech guys at Maddox Communications to hack into Melody's computer. After only five or six tries, he figured the password out all by himself. His birthday. The fact that it was something so simple surprised him a little, but he was grateful.

His first task was to remove evidence of Melody's affair from her computer, only she must have been very careful because he found nothing, not even a phone number or an entry in her calendar, that suggested she was sneaking around.

As for the baby, there were a few doctor appointments

listed on her calendar, and the history in her Internet browser showed visits to several children's furniture store sites and a site called Mom-to-be.com, where it appeared she had been tracking her pregnancy—she was fourteen weeks and four days on the day of the accident—and blogging on a page for single mothers.

Apparently she had every intention of doing this alone. Was it possible that the father of the baby was nothing more than a one-night stand? A glorified sperm donor?

He skimmed the entries she had written, hoping to find a clue as to who the man was, or the circumstances surrounding their relationship. But after more than an hour of reading, all he'd learned was that the baby's father was, in her words, *not involved*. He noted that some of the earlier posts dated back to the weeks before she left him. It was also clear, by the tone of her posts, that she was very excited to be a mother, which surprised him.

She had always been so independent and career focused, he didn't think she even wanted a family. Of course, that was never something they talked about. Maybe because she knew that if she wanted children, she wouldn't be having them with him. Not naturally anyway. Knowing that he couldn't father a child of his own, he'd resigned himself to the idea of not having them at all.

What he found even more disturbing than the information about the baby was a file folder with electronic copies of her report cards. They dated back the past four semesters. Whenever Ash asked her about school, which admittedly wasn't very often, Mel claimed things were going great. Which was hard to believe now that he saw that she had been clinging to a low C average, when he knew for a fact that in her first year she'd never scored anything lower than an A minus.

It was as if she had lost her interest in the law. But if that was the case, why hadn't she said anything? It was true that they didn't normally talk about those kinds of things, but going to school for a career she no longer wanted seemed worth mentioning. Especially when he was shelling out the money for her tuition.

The more Ash looked through her files and read her e-mails, the more he began to realize that after three years together, he barely knew Melody. She lived a life that, outside the bedroom, had little to do with him. And though that was the way he'd always wanted it, he couldn't help but feel…indignant. And maybe a little angry with himself for not taking the time to get to know her better.

He may have been there for her financially, but even he had to admit that emotionally, he'd been pretty much vacant.

Which was exactly what they had agreed to going into this relationship, so he had no absolutely no reason to feel as though he had wronged her somehow.

If that was true, why did he feel like such a jerk?

Maybe his ex was right. Maybe he'd been too cold and distant. Maybe he used work as an escape from dealing with the ups and downs of his personal relationships. And maybe, like his ex-wife, Melody had grown tired of the distance. Tired of being alone.

Regardless of what she felt, that was no excuse to be unfaithful. If she wanted more, she should have leveled with him. Although for the life of him, he wasn't sure what he would have told her. If she had given him an ultimatum—a real relationship or she would find someone new—would he have been able to just let her go? A real relationship just seemed like so much work. More than he had time for.

But he was here now, wasn't he? He had *made* the time for this. Didn't that tell him something?

Sure it did, he just wasn't sure what. But he knew that at some point he was going to have to figure it out. Maybe it was simply that being with Melody had been very easy, and he wasn't quite ready to give that up.

Unfortunately, remembering how good things had been made her betrayal sting that much more.

Just as he promised, Ash was back at the hospital as soon as visiting hours began the next morning. He was dressed casually this time, in slacks and a silk, button-down shirt. And she could tell, as he walked into the room, a sly grin on his face, that he was holding something behind his back. Probably flowers.

"Wow, you look great," he said, and she knew he wasn't just saying it to be nice because the nurse had said the same thing.

"I feel really good," she admitted, and she was pretty sure it had a lot to do with him. Before he came to see her yesterday she had felt so depressed and alone. As though she had nothing to look forward to, no reason to get better. Everything was different now. She was engaged to be married, and had a home to return to. A whole life to explore and relearn. What more could she ask for?

"I got my appetite back in a big way. I just finished breakfast and I'm already anxious for lunch. Although I have to say, the food here leaves a lot to be desired."

"There's a diner a few blocks from here that has decent food. Maybe I can pick you up something for lunch, if it's okay with your doctor."

"I'll make sure the nurse asks him. I could go for a big juicy burger and greasy French fries."

"I didn't know you liked burgers and fries."

"What do I usually eat?"

"Salads and chicken mostly. Occasionally you'll have

red meat, but not more than once a week. You've always been extremely health conscious."

"Well, I keep seeing these fast-food ads and every time they show a burger my mouth starts to water. I'll worry about being health conscious when I'm out of the hospital." Which was a completely backward way of looking at it, she realized, but she didn't even care. Eating like a rabbit wouldn't build her strength and get her the heck out of here.

"A burger and fries it is then," he said, and he was still hiding whatever it was he was holding behind his back.

"So, are you going to show me what you've got there, or make me guess?" she asked.

"You mean this?" he asked, his smile widening as he pulled a laptop from behind him.

"Is that mine?" she asked and he nodded. "I thought it was password protected. Did you talk to the guys at work already?"

He set it in her lap. "I didn't have to. I made a few educated guesses and figured it out for myself."

She squealed with excitement. "Oh, my gosh! You're my hero!"

He regarded her quizzically, as if she had just said something totally off the wall.

"What?" she asked. "Why are you looking at me like that?"

"Sorry. I just never imagined you as the kind of a woman who would have a hero. You're far too self-sufficient."

"Well, I do now," she said with a smile. "And it's you."

She opened the laptop and pressed the button to boot it up, relieved that at least she recalled how. When the password screen popped up, she looked to Ash.

"Type in one, one, nineteen, seventy-five."

"What is it?"

"My birthday."

I guess it made sense that she would use her fiancé's birthday as a password. Unless she didn't want him getting into her files, which obviously wasn't an issue. She typed the digits in and the system screen popped up. "It worked!"

"You remember how to use it?"

She nodded. Like so many other things, navigating the computer just seemed to come naturally. She only hoped that the information it contained would spark other memories. Personal memories.

"I'm going to head down to the gift store and see if they have a *Wall Street Journal*," Ash said, and Melody nodded, only half listening as she began opening files on her desktop. "If they don't, I might try to find one at the party store around the block."

"'Kay," she said. "Take your time."

She started with her e-mail, thinking saved messages would hold the most information, but there weren't many. And of the dozen or so, most were from Ash. It seemed a little strange, especially being in school, that she didn't have more, but it was always possible she kept them on an off-site server for safekeeping. Especially if they were for her supposed research, and were of a high security nature.

Or maybe her imagination was getting the best of her again.

She opened her calendar next, going back for several months, and found nothing but her school schedule, a few theater and party dates with Ash, and of course her research trip, which according to this should have ended a few days after her accident. She also found a recent appointment with a wedding planner that they had missed, and realized that not only were they engaged, but apparently they had already set a date. One they would probably be forced to postpone now.

She quit out of her calendar and opened her photo file, but either she kept her pictures online or on a disk, or she wasn't a very sentimental person, because there were very few. Shots of herself and Ash, mostly. None of friends or fellow students. And none of family, which was no surprise since she didn't have any.

She did have a vast music library, and while she liked the various songs she sampled, she didn't relate them to any specific memories or events.

She went through file after file, but not a single thing, not even her school papers, looked familiar to her. She tried to be logical about it. She had barely been out of her coma for four days and the doctor had said it would take time. *Logically* she knew this, and she was trying to heed his advice. Emotionally though, she felt like putting her fist through the nearest wall.

"I hope you're not doing schoolwork already!" the nurse said as she walked in to check Melody's IV. Which was kind of a ridiculous notion, since not only would Melody not have a clue what work had been assigned, but even if she did, she wouldn't have any idea how to do it. She didn't remember anything about the law. But she had to cut the nurse some slack. It probably wasn't often she dealt with amnesia patients.

"I'm just looking at photos and things," Melody told her. "I was hoping I would remember something."

"That's a great idea! How's it going?"

"Nothing so far."

She hung a fresh IV bag and tossed the empty one in the trash by the sink. "Dr. Nelson would like to see you up and moving around today. But only with assistance," she added sternly.

Melody wouldn't dare try it alone. When she'd taken her shower earlier the nurse had to help her, and she had to shower sitting down. Her legs felt like limp spaghetti noodles and she was so dizzy she was having trouble staying upright.

"We could take a few practice steps right now," the nurse suggested, a not-so-subtle nudge, but Melody wasn't quite ready to put her computer aside.

"Could we maybe do it after lunch?" she asked.

"All right, but don't put it off too long. You need to rebuild your strength."

Melody knew that better than everyone else. And though walking might still be a challenge, she could feel herself improving by leaps and bounds. She gave most of the credit to Ash.

He'd given her something to fight for.

Five

After the nurse left, Melody went back to the photo file on her computer and opened a few of herself and Ash. When she looked at herself, it was still a bit like looking at a stranger. It was her, but not exactly her.

Her clothes were obviously expensive and quite form-fitting. The healthy eating must have paid off because she was very trim and fit—although now, after being in the coma, she looked a little gaunt. She seemed to like to show off her cleavage, which admittedly she had a fair amount of. She peeked under her hospital gown at her breasts and decided that she must own some pretty amazing push-up bras.

In the photos her hair was always fixed in a sleek and chic style that she couldn't help thinking must have taken ages in front of the bathroom mirror to perfect. So unlike the casual, wavy locks she was sporting now. Also, she wore a considerable amount of makeup and it was always flawlessly applied. She looked very well put together.

Just the thought of the time it must have taken to get ready each morning left her feeling exhausted. Maybe, when she was up and around again, she would feel differently. Although she couldn't help thinking she looked a bit...*vain*. But she was sure these photos represented only a small segment of her life. Who didn't like to look good for pictures? And she couldn't deny that she and Ash made one heck of a good-looking couple.

How would he feel if she didn't go back to being that perfectly put together woman? Would he be disappointed? Or did he love her for the woman inside?

The latter, she hoped. If not, would he be here by her side while she healed?

"Still at it?" the man in question said, and she looked up to find him standing at the foot of the bed. Ash was holding a newspaper in one hand and a brown paper sack in the other.

"You're back already?" she asked.

"Already? I've been gone almost two hours."

"Has it really been that long?" She would have guessed twenty-five or thirty minutes.

"I had to make a few calls to work, and I figured you wouldn't mind the time alone. Which apparently you didn't." He nodded to her computer. "Any luck?"

She closed the computer and shook her head, trying not to let it discourage her, or to dwell on it. "I've looked at pretty much all of it and I don't recognize a thing." She gestured to the bag he was holding. "What's that?"

"I stopped at the nurses' station on my way out this morning, and they called the doctor, who said there's no reason to have you on a restricted diet, so..." He pulled a white foam restaurant container from the bag. "Your burger and fries, madam."

The scent of the food wafted her way and her mouth instantly started to water. Now she knew why she was marrying Ash. He was clearly the sweetest man in the world.

"You're wonderful!" she said as he set it on her tray. "I can see why I fell in love with you."

He gave her another one of those funny looks, as though the sentiment was totally unexpected or out of character.

"What? Don't tell me I've never said I love you."

"It's not that. I just…" He shook his head. "I just didn't expect to hear anything like that so soon. I guess I figured you would have to take the time to get to know me again."

"Well, I sure like what I've seen so far." She opened the container top, her taste buds going berserk in anticipation. Her stomach growled and, up until that instant, she didn't even realize she was hungry. She automatically grabbed a packet of ketchup, tore it open with her teeth, and drizzled it over her fries. Ash pulled out a similar container for himself and set it beside hers on the tray, but his was a BLT with coleslaw. He sat on the edge of the mattress near her to eat.

The fries were greasy and salty, and by far the best thing Melody had eaten in days. Or maybe *ever*. And when she took a bite of her burger it was pure nirvana.

"How did your calls to work go?" she asked. "Are they upset that you'll be gone for a while?"

He shrugged. "Doesn't matter how they feel. They don't have a say in the matter."

She frowned. "I would feel awful if I got you in trouble, or even worse, if you got fired because of me."

"Don't worry. They aren't going to fire me. I'm the

best damned CFO they've ever had. Besides, they know that if they did let me go, their competitor, Golden Gate Promotions, would probably snap me up. The owner, Athos Koteas, would do just about anything for an edge. And that would be very bad for Maddox."

"Not if your contract has a noncompete clause," she said, stuffing a fry in her mouth. "Working for a competitor would be a direct breach. They could sue the pants off you. And I'm sure they would."

When she glanced up, Ash had gone still with his sandwich halfway to his mouth, and he was giving her that "look" again. Why did he keep doing that? "*What?* Do I have ketchup on my face or something?"

"Mel, do you realize what you just said?"

She hit rewind and ran it through her head again, stunned when the meaning of her words sank in. "I was talking like a lawyer."

Ash nodded.

"Oh, my gosh! I didn't even think about it. It just… popped out." A huge smile crept across her face. "I remembered something!"

Granted it was nothing important, or personal, but it was *something*. She tried to dredge up some other legal jargon, but her mind went blank. Maybe that was just the way it was going to be. Maybe it would come back in little bits and pieces. At that rate she would have her full memory back by the time she and Ash retired, she thought wryly.

"For the record," he said, "I did have a noncompete clause and they removed it when I refused to sign."

Maybe it was her imagination, but she had the feeling Ash didn't share in her happiness. It was as if he thought her remembering something was a *bad* thing.

It was just one more little thing that seemed…off.

She shook the thought away. She was being ridiculous.

Of course he wanted her to remember things. Didn't he? What reason would he have not to?

That, she realized, was what she needed to find out.

That had been a close call, Ash thought as he and Mel ate lunch. In hindsight, bringing her computer might not have been the brightest idea he'd ever had, but doing it today, instead of waiting until they got back to San Francisco, had sort of been an accident. He'd grabbed it on his way out the door when he left for the hospital. He didn't like the idea of leaving it in the room, for fear that it might be stolen. But as he climbed into his rental, the interior, at nine in the morning, was already about a million degrees. Assuming he would be in the hospital most of the day, it didn't seem wise to leave the laptop in the car, in the blistering heat.

What choice did he have but to bring it into the hospital with him, and as a result, give it to Melody? What if it did spark a memory? Was he willing to jeopardize his plans? He'd been up half the night removing personal information, so it seemed unlikely anything would shake loose a memory.

To confuse her, and hopefully buy himself a little more time, he not only removed things from the computer, but *added* a few things, as well.

To give her the impression they attended social functions together—when in reality they rarely went out socially—he added a few entries for fictional theater dates and parties. He also included a meeting with a wedding planner, which he thought was a nice touch. One they had regretfully missed because Mel had been missing.

The most brilliant switch, in his opinion, was her music. He knew from experience that some songs evoked specific memories or feelings. Like the knot he got in his stomach whenever he heard "Hey Jude" by the Beatles, the song that was playing the day he drove home to break the good news about his promotion and found his ex in bed with her personal trainer.

So, he deleted Mel's entire music catalog and replaced it with his own music library. Mel had always preferred current pop music, while he listened to classic rock and jazz. There wasn't much chance that would be jogging any memories.

Now he was wondering if that hadn't been enough. Or maybe the memories were going to come back regardless. Either way, he didn't want to panic prematurely. Remembering something about the law was still a far cry from regaining her personal memories.

He looked over at Melody and realized she'd stopped eating with nearly half her burger and fries still left.

"Full already?" he asked.

"Is there something you're not telling me?" she asked. "Something you don't want me to know?"

The question came so far out of left field he was struck dumb for several seconds, and when his brain finally kicked back in he figured it would be in his best interest to *play* dumb. "What do you mean?"

She pushed her tray aside. "I just get this nagging feeling that you're hiding something from me."

He could play this one of two ways. He could act angry and indignant, but in his experience that just screamed *guilty*. So instead he went for the wounded angle.

He pasted on a baffled expression and said, "God, Mel, why would you think that? If I did or said something to hurt your feelings…" He shrugged helplessly.

The arrow hit its mark. Melody looked crushed.

"Of course you haven't. You've been wonderful." She reached out and put her hand on his forearm. "You've done so much for me and I'm acting completely ungrateful. Just forget I said anything."

He laid his hand over hers and gave it a squeeze. "You suffered a severe head injury. You were in a coma for two weeks." He flashed her a sympathetic smile. "I promise I won't hold it against you."

Her smile was a grateful one. And of course, he felt like slime for playing on her emotions. For using it to his advantage.

Remember what she did to you, he told himself. Although, one thing he couldn't deny was that Melody was not the woman she'd been before the accident. In the past, she *never* would have confronted him this way with her suspicions. Yet, at the same time, she was much softer and compassionate than she used to be. Not to mention uncharacteristically open with her emotions.

When she told him she loved him he'd felt…well, he honestly wasn't sure *what* he'd felt. It was just…unusual. No one had said that to him in a long time. He and his wife had stopped expressing sentiments of love long before the final meltdown. The pain of their breakup had been less about lost love than the humiliation of her deceit, and his own stupidity for not seeing her for what she really was.

In the long run he honestly believed she had done him a favor, although he could have done without seeing the proof with his own eyes.

Even if Melody thought she loved Ash, she obviously didn't mean it or she wouldn't have cheated on him in the first place. Besides, their relationship wasn't about love. It was more about mutual respect and convenience. She was only saying what she thought she was *supposed* to say. She probably just assumed that she would never be engaged to a man she didn't love. But that was all part of the plan, wasn't it? To make her believe that they were in love. And apparently it was working.

He couldn't deny that in her current condition, he was having a tough time keeping a grip on the anger he'd felt when he learned about her pregnancy. He was sure that once he got her back home and she started acting like her old self, the wounds would feel fresh again. He would approach the situation with a renewed sense of vengeance.

He was counting on it.

Six days after Ash arrived in Abilene, after showing what Dr. Nelson said was remarkable progress, Melody was finally released from the hospital. An orderly wheeled her down to the front entrance, her heart pounding in anticipation of finally being free, and as they exited the building, a wall of hot, dry air washed over her.

She hoped their place in San Francisco had a courtyard or a balcony, because after being cooped up in the hospital for so long, she wanted to spend lots of time outside. She closed her eyes and breathed in deep, felt the sun beat down hot on her face as she was wheeled from under the awning to the curb where Ash waited with his rental car. It was barely 10:00 a.m. and it had to be pushing ninety degrees. The sun was so bright, she had to raise a hand to shade her eyes. She wasn't sure of the make of the vehicle, but it looked expensive.

Ash had dressed casually for the trip, in jeans and a T-shirt, and Melody didn't miss the group of nurses following him with their eyes, practically drooling on their scrubs.

Look all you like ladies, but he's mine.

Not that Melody blamed them for gawking. He looked hot as hell dressed that way. The shirt accentuated the width of his shoulders and showed off the lean muscle in his arms, and the jeans hugged his behind in a way that gave her impure thoughts. She could hardly wait until she was feeling well enough to have sex again. Right now, if she did anything marginally taxing, her head began to pound.

As soon as they reached the car Ash opened the door. A rush of cool air cut through the heat as he helped her from the chair to the front seat. The interior was soft black leather, and it had what looked like a top-of-the-line sound and navigation system. Ash got her settled in and helped with her seat belt, and as he leaned over her to fasten it, he smelled so delicious she wanted to bury her face in the crook of his neck and take a nibble. When he seemed convinced she was securely fastened in, with her seat as far back as it would go—just in case the airbag deployed and bonked her head, rattling her already compromised brain—he walked around and got in the driver's side. "Are you ready?" he asked.

"I am *so* ready."

He turned the key and the engine hummed to life, and as he pulled from the curb and down the driveway toward the road, she had this odd feeling of urgency. She felt that if he didn't hurry, the staff members were going to change their minds and chase her down like a fugitive, or an escaped mental patient, and make her go back to that awful room.

It wasn't until he pulled out onto the main road and hit the gas, and the hospital finally disappeared out of sight, that she could breathe easy again. She was finally free. As long as she lived, she hoped she never had to stay in a hospital room again.

He glanced over at her. "You all right?"

"I am now."

"You're comfortable?" he asked.

"Very." He'd brought her suitcase to the hospital and she'd chosen a pair of jeans and a cotton shirt to start the trip. She'd tried to find a bra she liked, but either they were push-up and squeezed her breasts to within an inch of her life or they were made of itchy lace, so she'd opted not to wear one at all. As long as she didn't get cold, or pull her shirt taut, it was kind of hard to tell. Besides, it was just her and Ash and he'd seen her breasts plenty of times before.

The jeans were comfortable, and although at one point she was guessing they were pretty tight, now they hung off her. Despite her constant cravings for food, her eyes were bigger than her stomach, but Dr. Nelson assured her that her appetite would return.

She'd opted to wear flip-flops on her feet and toed them off the instant she was in the car, keeping them within reach should she happen to need them.

Other than the dull ache in her temples, she couldn't be more comfortable.

"If you need to stop for any reason just let me know," Ash told her. "And if the driving gets to be too much we'll stop and get a hotel room."

"I'm sure I'll be fine." If it were at all possible, she wished they could drive straight through until they got to San Francisco, but it was a twenty-four-hour trip and she knew Ash would have to sleep at some point. Still, she wanted to stay on the road as long as possible. The sooner they got home, the better. She was convinced that once she was there, surrounded by her own possessions, her memories would begin to return.

Ash turned onto the I-20 on-ramp, hit the gas and zoomed onto the freeway, shooting like a rocket into traffic.

"This is pretty nice for a rental," she told him.

"It's not a rental," he said as he maneuvered left into the fast lane. "This is my car."

His car? "I thought you flew here."

"I did, but I wanted you to be comfortable on the way home so I arranged to have my car brought to Texas. It arrived yesterday morning."

That couldn't have been cheap. She'd never asked Ash about their financial situation, but apparently CFOs at San Francisco ad agencies made decent money.

"It looks expensive," she said. "The car, I mean."

He shrugged. "I like nice cars."

"So I guess you do okay? Financially."

He flashed her a side glance, one of those funny looks that had become so familiar this past week. "Are you asking how much I make?"

"No! Of course not. It's just, well…you wear expensive clothes and drive an expensive car. So I'm assuming you make a decent living, that's all."

"I do okay," he said, a grin kicking up one corner of his mouth, as though the idea of her even asking amused him. And she knew that if she asked exactly how much he made, he would probably tell her. It just wasn't that important.

All that mattered to her was how wonderful he'd been this week. Other than running an occasional errand, or stepping out to pick up food, Ash hadn't left her side. He got there every morning after visiting hours started and didn't leave until they ended at ten. She had been off her feet for so long and her muscles had deteriorated so much that at first walking had been a challenge. Because she was determined to get out of there as soon as humanly possible, Melody had paced, back and forth, up and down the corridors for hours to build her strength. And Ash had been right there by her side.

At first, she'd literally needed him there to hang on to, or to lean on when her balance got hinky. It was frustrating, not being able to do something as simple as taking a few steps unassisted, but Ash kept pumping her full of encouragement and, after the second day, she could manage with only her IV pole to steady her. When they finally removed her IV, she'd been a little wary at first, but realized she was steady enough walking without it. Yesterday she had been chugging along at a pretty good pace when Dr. Nelson came by to let her know she would be released in the morning. He had already discussed her case with a neurologist in San Francisco—one of the best, he said—and Melody would go in to see him as soon as they were home.

Melody's lids started to feel droopy and she realized the pain pills the nurse had given her right before she was discharged were starting to kick in.

Ash must have noticed because he said, "Why don't you put your seat back? It's the lever on the right. And there's a pillow and blanket in the backseat if you need them."

The man thought of *everything*.

It was plenty warm in the car, even with the air on, but the pillow sounded good. She reclined her seat then grabbed the pillow from the back and tucked it under her head. She sighed and snuggled into the buttery-soft leather, sure that her hospital bed hadn't been half as comfortable. She wanted to stay awake, to keep Ash company, but her lids just didn't want to cooperate, so finally she stopped fighting it and let them close. It couldn't have been ten seconds before she slipped into a deep, dreamless sleep.

Six

Melody woke, disoriented and confused, expecting to be in her hospital bed. The she remembered she'd been set free and smiled, even though her head ached so hard she was sure that her eyeballs were going to pop from their sockets.

"Have a good nap?"

She looked over and saw Ash gazing down at her, a bottle of soda in his hand. Only then did she realize they were no longer moving. She rubbed her eyes, giving them a gentle push inward, just in case, and asked, "Why are we stopped?"

"Lunch break."

She looked up and saw that they were parked in a fast-food restaurant lot.

"I was just going in to grab a burger. Do you want anything?"

"No, I'm good. But my head is pounding. What time is it?"

"After three."

She'd been asleep for *five* hours?

"It's probably the elevation. Do you need a pain pill?"

She nodded, so he opened the glove box and pulled out the prescription they had filled at the hospital pharmacy. "One or two?"

One pill wouldn't put her to sleep, and she would be able to keep Ash company, but gauging the pain in her head, she needed two. "Two, I think."

He tapped them out of the bottle and offered his soda to wash them down. "I'm going in. You sure you don't want anything?"

"I'm sure."

While he was gone she lay back and closed her eyes. She must have drifted off again because when the car door opened, it startled her awake.

Ash was back with a bag of food. He unwrapped his burger in his lap and set his fries in the console cup holder. It wasn't until they were back on the highway, and the aroma permeated the interior, when her stomach started to rumble in protest.

Maybe she was hungry after all. Every time he took a bite her jaw tightened and her mouth watered.

After a while Ash asked, "Is there a reason you're watching me eat?"

She didn't realize how intently she'd been staring. "Um, no?"

"You wouldn't be hungry, would you?" he asked.

She was starving, but she couldn't very well ask him to turn around and go back. "I can wait until the next stop."

"Look in the bag," he told her.

She did, and found another burger and fries inside.

"I kind of figured once you saw me eating you would be hungry, too."

"Just one more reason why I love you," she said, diving into her food with gusto.

She was only able to eat about half, so Ash polished off the rest. When she was finished eating the painkillers had kicked in and she dozed off with her stomach pleasantly full. A few hours later she roused for a trip to the rest stop, and as soon as the car was moving again, promptly fell back to sleep. The next time she opened her eyes it was dark and they were parked in front of an economy hotel. She realized that Ash was standing outside the open passenger door, his hand was on her shoulder, and he was nudging her awake.

"What time is it?" she asked groggily.

"After eleven. We're stopping for the night," he said. "I got us a room."

Thirteen hours down, eleven to go, she thought. Maybe this time tomorrow they would be home.

He helped her out and across the parking lot. All the sleep should have energized her, but she was still exhausted, and her head hurt worse than it had before. Maybe this trip was harder on her system than she realized.

Their bags were already inside and sitting on the bed.

"They didn't have any doubles left and there isn't another hotel for miles," he said apologetically. "If you don't want to share, I can sack out on the floor."

They had shared a bed for *three* years. Of course, she had no memory of that. Maybe he was worried that she would feel strange sleeping with him until they got to know one another better. Which she had to admit was pretty sweet. It was a little unusual being with him this late at night, since he always left the hospital by ten. But actually, it was kind of nice.

"I don't mind sharing," she assured him.

"How's your head feel?"

She rubbed her left temple. "Like it's going to implode. Or explode. I'm not sure which."

He tapped two painkillers out and got her a glass of water. "Maybe a hot shower would help."

She swallowed them and said, "It probably would."

"You can use the bathroom first."

She stepped in the bathroom and closed the door, smiling when she saw that he'd set her toiletry bag on the edge of the sink. He seriously could not take better care of her.

She dropped her clothes on the mat and blasted the water as hot as she could stand then stepped under the spray. She soaped up, then washed and conditioned her hair, then she closed her eyes and leaned against the wall, letting the water beat down on her. When she felt herself listing to one side her eyes flew open and she jerked upright, realizing that she had actually drifted off to sleep.

She shut the water off and climbed out, wrapping herself in a towel that reeked of bleach. She combed her hair and brushed her teeth, grabbed her dirty clothes, and when she stepped out of the bathroom Ash was lying in bed with the television controller in one hand, watching a news program.

"Your turn," she said.

He glanced over at her, did a quick double take, then turned back to the TV screen. "I thought I was going to have to call in the national guard," he said. "You were in there a while."

"Sorry. I fell asleep in the shower."

"On or off?" he said, gesturing to the TV.

"Off. The second my head hits the pillow I'll be out cold."

He switched it off and rolled out of bed, grabbing the pajama bottoms he'd set out. "Out in a minute," he said as he stepped in the bathroom and shut the door. Less than ten seconds later she heard the shower turn on.

Barely able to keep her eyes open, Melody walked on wobbly legs to the bed. She'd forgotten to grab something to sleep in from her suitcase, and with her case on the floor across the room, it hardly seemed worth the effort. It wasn't as if he had never seen her naked before, and if she was okay with it, she was sure he would be, too.

She dropped her towel on the floor and climbed under the covers, her mind going soft and fuzzy as the painkillers started to do their job.

At some point she heard the bathroom door open and heard Ash moving around in the room, then she felt the covers shift, and she could swear she heard Ash curse under his breath. It seemed as though it was a long time before she felt the bed sink under his weight, or maybe it was just her mind playing tricks on her. But finally she felt him settle into bed, his arm not much more than an inch from her own, its heat radiating out to touch her.

She drifted back to sleep and woke in the darkness with something warm and smooth under her cheek. It took a second to realize that it was Ash's chest. He was flat on his back and she was lying draped across him. At some point she must have cuddled up to him. She wondered if they slept like this all the time. She hoped so, because she liked it. It felt nice to be so close to him.

The next time she woke up, she could see the hint of sunlight through a break in the curtains. She was still lying on Ash, her leg thrown over one of his, and his arm was looped around her, his hand resting on her bare hip.

The covers had slipped down just low enough for her to see the tent in his pajama bottoms. It looked…well…*big,* and for the first time since the accident she felt the honest-to-goodness tug of sexual arousal. She suddenly became ultra-aware of her body pressed against his. Her nipples pulled into two hard points and started to tingle, until it felt as though the only relief would come from rubbing them against his warm skin. In fact, she had the urge to rub her entire body all over his. She arched her back, drawing his leg deeper between her thighs, and as she did, her thigh brushed against his erection. He groaned in his sleep and sank his fingers into the flesh of her hip. Tingles of desire shivered straight through to her core.

It felt so good to be touched, and she wanted more; unfortunately, the more turned on she became, and the faster her blood raced through her veins, the more her head began to throb. She took a deep breath to calm her hammering heart. It was clear that it would be a while before she was ready to put her body through the stress of making love.

That didn't make her want Ash any less, and it didn't seem fair to make him keep waiting, after having already gone through months of abstinence, when there was no reason why she couldn't make him feel good.

Didn't she owe him for being so good to her? For sticking by her side?

Melody looked at the tent in his pajamas, imagined putting her hand inside, and was hit with a sudden and overwhelming urge to touch him, a need to please him that seemed to come from somewhere deep inside, almost like a shadowy memory, hazy and distant and just out of reach. It had never occurred to her before, but maybe being intimate with him would jog her memory.

She slid her hand down his taut and warm stomach,

under the waistband of his pajama bottoms. She felt the muscle just below the skin contract and harden under her touch. She moved lower still, tunneling her fingers through the wiry hair at the base. He was so warm there, as if all the heat in his body had trickled down to pool in that one spot.

She played there for just a few seconds, drawing her fingers back and forth through his hair, wondering what was going on in his head. Other than the tensing of his abdomen and the slight wrinkle between his brows, he appeared to be sleeping soundly.

When the anticipation became too much, she slid her hand up and wrapped it around his erection. The months without sex must have taken their toll because he was rock hard, and as she stroked her way upward, running her thumb along the tip, it was already wet and slippery.

She couldn't recall ever having done this before—though she was sure she had, probably more times than she could count—but she inherently seemed to know what to do, knew what he liked. She kept her grip firm and her pace slow and even, and Ash seemed to like it. She could see the blood pulsing at the base of his throat and his hips started to move in time with her strokes. She looked up, watching his face. She could tell he was beginning to wake up, and she wanted to see his expression when he did.

His breath was coming faster now and his head thrashed from one side to the other, then back again. She was sure that all he needed was one little push…

She turned her face toward his chest, took his nipple in her mouth, then bit down. Not hard enough to leave a mark, only to arouse, and it worked like a charm. A groan ripped from Ash's chest and his hips bucked upward, locking as his body let go. His fingers dug into her flesh, then he relaxed and went slack beneath her.

Mel looked up at him and found that he was looking back at her, drowsy and a little disoriented, as if he were still caught somewhere between asleep and awake. He looked down at her hand still gripping him inside his pajamas. She waited for the smile to curl his mouth, for him to tell her how good she made him feel, but instead he frowned and snapped, "Mel, what are you doing?"

Mel snatched her hand from inside Ash's pajamas, grabbed the sheet and yanked it up to cover herself. He couldn't tell if she was angry or hurt, or a little of both. But Melody didn't do angry. Not with him anyway. At least, she never *used* to.

"I think the appropriate thing to say at a time like this is thanks, that felt great," she snapped.

Yep, that was definitely anger.

"That did feel great. The part I was *awake* for." Which wasn't much.

He knew last night, when he'd pulled back the covers and discovered she was naked, that sleeping next to her would be a bad idea. When he woke in the middle of the night with her draped over him like a wet noodle, limp and soft and sleeping soundly, he knew that he should have rolled her over onto her own side of the bed, but he was too tired, and too comfortable to work up the will. And yeah, maybe it felt good, too. But he sure as hell hadn't expected to wake up this morning with her hand in his pants.

Before the accident it would have been par for the course. If he had a nickel for every time he'd roused in the morning in the middle of a hot dream to find Melody straddling him, or giving him head.

But now he almost felt…violated.

Looked as if he should have listened to his instincts and slept on the damned floor.

The worst thing about this was seeing her there barely covered with the sheet, one long, lithe leg peeking out from underneath, the luscious curve of her left breast exposed, her hair adorably mussed, and all he could think about was tossing her down on the mattress and having his way with her.

Sex with Melody had always been off-the-charts fantastic. *Always.* She had been willing to try anything at least once, and would go to practically any lengths to please him. In fact, there were times when she could be a little *too* adventurous and enthusiastic. Three years into their relationship they made love as often and as enthusiastically as their first time when it was all exciting and new—right up until the day she walked out on him.

But when it came to staying angry with her, seeing her in such a compromised condition and knowing that she had no recollection of cheating on him took some of the wind out of his sails. For now. When she got her memory back, that would be a whole other story.

But that did not mean he was ready to immediately hop back into bed with her. When, and *if,* he was ready to have sex with her, he would let her know. He was calling the shots this time.

"I don't get why you're so upset about this," she said, sounding indignant, and a little dejected.

"You could have woken me up and asked if it was okay."

"Well, seeing as how we're *engaged,* I really didn't think it would be a problem."

"You're not ready for sex."

"Which is why I don't expect anything from you. I was perfectly content just making you feel good. Most guys—"

"Most guys would not expect their fiancée, who just

suffered a serious head injury, to get them off. Especially one who's still too fragile to have him return the favor. Did you ever stop to think that I might feel guilty?"

Some of her anger fizzled away. "But it's been months for you, and I just thought…it just didn't seem fair."

Fair? "Okay, so it's been months. So what? I'm not a sex fiend. You may have noticed that my puny reptile brain functions just fine without it."

That made her crack a smile. "It didn't seem right that you had to suffer because of me. I just wanted to make you happy."

Is that what she had been doing the past three years? Making him happy? Had she believed that she needed to constantly please him sexually to keep him interested? Did she think that because he paid for her school, her room and board, kept her living a lifestyle many women would envy, that she was his…*sex slave?* And had he *ever* given her a reason to believe otherwise?

For him, their relationship was as much about companionship as sex. Although, in three years, of all the times she had offered herself so freely, not to mention enthusiastically, had he ever once stopped her and said, "Let's just talk instead?"

Was that why she cheated on him? Did she need someone who treated her like an equal and not a sex object?

If she felt that way, she should have said so. But since they were stuck together for a while, he should at least set the record straight.

"The thing is, Mel, I'm *not* suffering. And even if I was, you don't owe me anything."

"You sure looked like you were this morning when I woke up," she said.

"Mel, I'm a guy. I could be getting laid ten times a day

and I would still wake up with a hard-on. It's part of the outdoor plumbing package."

She smiled and he offered his hand for her to take. She had to let go of the sheet on one side and it dropped down, completely baring her left breast. It was firm and plump, her nipples small and rosy, and it took all the restraint he could muster not to lean forward and take her into his mouth. He realized he was staring and tore his gaze away to look in her eyes, but she'd seen, and he had the feeling she knew exactly what he'd been thinking.

"Not suffering, huh?" she said with a wry smile.

Well, not anymore. Not much anyway.

"I honestly believe that we need to take this slow," he said. "If you're not physically ready, we wait. *Both* of us."

"Okay," she agreed solemnly, giving his hand a squeeze. "You mind if I use the bathroom first, or do you want it?"

"Go ahead."

She rolled out of bed and he assumed she intended to take the sheet along to cover herself. Instead she let it fall and stood there in all her naked glory, thinner than she'd been, almost to point of looking a little bony, but still sexy and desirable as hell.

Instead of walking straight into the bathroom, she went the opposite way to her suitcase, her hair falling in mussed waves over her shoulders, the sway of her hips mesmerizing him. He expected her to lift her case and set it on the bed, but instead she bent at the waist to unzip her case right there. She stood not five feet away, her back to him, legs spread just far enough to give him a perfect view of her goods, and he damn near swallowed his own tongue. He saw two perfect globes of soft flesh that he was desperate to get his hands on, her thighs long and milky white, and what lay between them…damn. Doing him must have turned her on, too, because he could see traces of moisture glistening along her folds.

He had to fist the blankets to keep himself from reaching out and touching her. To stop himself from dropping to his knees and taking her into his mouth. He even caught himself licking his lips in anticipation.

She seemed to take an unnecessarily long time rifling through her clothes, choosing what to wear, then she straightened. He pulled the covers across his lap, so she wouldn't notice that conspicuous rise in his pajamas, but she didn't even look his way; then, as she stepped into the bathroom she tossed him a quick, wicked smile over her shoulder.

If that little display had been some sort of revenge for snapping at her earlier, she sure as hell knew how to hit where it stung.

Seven

They got back on the road late that morning—although it was Melody's own fault.

She'd already had a mild headache when she woke up, compounded by the sexual arousal, but bending over like that to open her case, and the pressure it had put on her head, had been a really bad move. The pain went from marginally cumbersome to oh-my-God-kill-me-now excruciating. But it had almost been worth it to see the look on Ash's face.

She popped two painkillers then got dressed, thinking she would lie down while Ash got ready then she would be fine. Unfortunately it was the kind of sick, throbbing pain that was nearly unbearable, and exacerbated by the tiniest movement.

Ash's first reaction was to drive her to the nearest hospital, but she convinced him that all she needed was a little quiet, and another hour or so of sleep. She urged him to go and get himself a nice breakfast, and wake her when he got back.

Instead, he let her sleep until almost eleven-thirty! It was nearly noon by the time they got on the road, and she realized, with a sinking heart, that they would never make it back to San Francisco that evening. On the bright side she managed to stay awake for most of the drive, and was able to enjoy the scenery as it passed. Ash played the radio and occasionally she would find herself singing along to songs she hadn't even realized she knew. But if she made a conscious effort to remember them, her stubborn brain refused to cooperate.

When they stopped for the night, this time it was in a much more populated area and he managed to find a higher-class hotel with two double beds. However, that didn't stop her from walking around naked and sleeping in the buff. The truth was, when it came to sleeping naked she wasn't really doing it to annoy Ash. She actually liked the feel of the sheets against her bare skin. The walking-around-naked part? That was just for fun.

Not that she didn't think Ash was right about waiting. When she'd invaded his pj's yesterday morning she really hadn't stopped to think that maybe he didn't want to, that he might feel guilty that it was one-sided. If she wanted to get technical, what she had done was tantamount to rape or molestation. Although, honestly, he hadn't seemed quite *that* scandalized.

Really, she should be thrilled that she was engaged to such a caring and sensitive man. And she supposed that if the burden of pent-up sexual energy became too much, he could just take care of matters himself. Although deep down she really hoped he would wait for her.

Despite wishing she was in Ash's bed, curled up against him, she got a decent night's sleep and woke feeling the

best she had since this whole mess began. Her head hardly
hurt and when they went to breakfast she ate every bite
of her waffles and sausage. Maybe just knowing that in
a few hours she would be home was all the medicine she
needed for a full recovery.

Ash spent a lot of the drive on the phone with work, and
though she wasn't sure exactly what was being discussed,
the tone of the conversation suggested that they were
relieved he was coming back. And he seemed happy to
be going back.

They crossed the Bay Bridge shortly after one, and they
were finally in San Francisco. Though the views were
gorgeous, she couldn't say with any certainty that it looked
the least bit familiar. They drove along the water, and
after only a few minutes Ash pulled into the underground
parking of a huge renovated warehouse that sat directly
across the street from a busy pier.

He never said anything about them living on the
water.

"Home sweet home," he said, zooming past a couple
dozen cars that looked just as classy as his, then he whipped
into a spot right next to the elevator.

She peered out the window. "So this is it?"

"This is the place." He opened his door and stuck one
foot out.

"What floor do we live on?"

"The top."

"What floor is that?"

"Six." He paused a second and asked, "Would you like
to go up?"

She did and she didn't. She had been anticipating this
day for what felt like ages, but now that she was here,
back to her old life, she was terrified. What if she didn't

remember? What if the memories never resurfaced? Who would she be?

Stop being such a baby, she chastised herself. Like Dr. Nelson had reminded her the day she was discharged, it was just going to take time and she would have to be patient. No matter what happened up there, whether she remembered or not, it was going to be okay. She was a fighter.

She turned to Ash and flashed him a shaky smile. "I'm ready."

She got out and waited by the elevator while Ash collected their bags from the trunk. He pushed the button for the elevator and it immediately opened. They stepped inside and he slipped a key in a lock on the panel, then hit the button for the top floor.

"Does everyone need a key?" she asked.

He shook his head. "Only our floor."

She wondered why, and how many other condos were on the top floor. She was going to ask, but the movement of the elevator made her so dizzy it was all she could do to stay upright. Besides, as the elevator came to a stop and the doors slid open, she got her answer.

They stepped off the elevator not into a hallway, but in a small vestibule in front of a set of double doors. Doors that led directly into their condo! They weren't a condo on the sixth floor. They *were* the sixth floor, and what she saw inside when he unlocked the door literally took her breath away. The entire living area—kitchen, dining room and family room—was one huge open space with a ceiling two stories high, bordered by a wall of windows that overlooked the ocean.

The floors were mahogany, with a shine so deep she could see herself in it. The kitchen looked ultramodern and she was guessing it had every device and gadget on the market. The furniture looked trendy but comfortable, and everything, from the oriental rugs to light fixtures, screamed top-of-the-line.

For a second she just stood there frozen, wondering if, as some sick joke, he'd taken her to someone else's condo. If they really lived here, how could she *not* remember it?

Ash set the bags on the floor and dropped his keys on a trendy little drop-leaf table beside the door. He started to walk toward the kitchen, but when he realized she wasn't moving, he stopped and turned to her. "Are you coming in?"

"You told me you do okay," she said, and at his confused look she added, "financially. But you do *way* better than okay, don't you?"

He grinned and said, "A little bit better than okay."

Her fiancé was loaded. She lived in a loft condo overlooking the ocean. It was almost too much to take in all at once. "Why didn't you tell me?"

He shrugged. "It just didn't seem that important. And I didn't want to overwhelm you."

"Oh, awesome idea, because I'm not the least bit overwhelmed *now!*" She was so freaked out she was practically hyperventilating.

"I take it nothing looks familiar."

"Curiously, no. And you'd think I would have remembered *this.*"

"Why don't I show you around?"

She nodded and followed him to the kitchen, looking out the bank of windows as they passed, and the view was so breathtaking she had to stop. She could see sailboats and ships on the water and they had a phenomenal view of the Bay Bridge.

Ash stepped up behind her. "Nice view, huh?"

"It's...*amazing.*"

"That's why I bought this place. I always wanted a place by the water."

"How long have you lived here?"

"I bought it after the divorce was final. Right before we met. You've lived here almost as long as I have. You've always said that your favorite room is the kitchen."

She could see why. The cabinets had a mahogany base with frosted glass doors; the countertops were black granite. All the appliances, even the coffeemaker, were stainless steel and it looked as functional as it was aesthetically pleasing. "Do I cook?"

"You're an excellent cook."

She hoped that was one of those things that just came naturally.

There was a laundry room and half bath behind the kitchen, then they moved on to the bedrooms, which were sectioned off on the right side of the loft. Three huge rooms, each with its own full bath and an enormous walk-in closet. He used one as a home office, one was the master, and the third he told her was hers.

"We don't share?" she asked, trying hard to disguise her disappointment.

"Well, you've always used this as an office and kept your clothes and things in here. I just figured that until things settle down, maybe you should sleep here, too."

But what if she wanted to sleep with him?

He's only thinking of your health, she assured herself. She knew that if they slept in the same bed they would be tempted to do things that she just was not ready for. Look what had happened in the hotel. And last night she had wanted so badly to climb out of her own bed and slip into his.

She walked over to the closet and stepped inside, looking at all of her belongings. She ran her hands over the shirts and slacks and dresses, feeling the soft, expensive fabrics, disheartened by how unfamiliar it all was.

"Well?" Ash asked, leaning in the closet doorway, looking so casually sexy in faded jeans and an untucked, slightly rumpled polo shirt, his hair stilled mussed from driving with the windows down, that she had the bone-deep feeling that as long as they had each other, everything would be okay.

"They're nice clothes, but I don't recognize them."

"It'll come to you, just—"

"Be patient, I know. I'm trying."

"What are you planning to do now?"

"Look through my things, I guess. It's weird, but it feels almost like I'll be snooping."

"If it's okay with you," he said, "I'm going to go to the office for a while."

They'd barely been back ten minutes and already he was going to leave her alone? "But we just got here."

"I know, but I'll only be a couple of hours," he assured her. "You'll be fine. Why don't you relax and take some time familiarizing yourself with the condo. And you look like you could use a nap."

She didn't want him to go, but he had sacrificed so much already for her. It was selfish to think that he didn't deserve to get back to his life. And hadn't the doctor suggested she try to get back into her regular routine as soon as possible?

"You're right," she told Ash. "I'll be fine."

"Get some rest. Oh, and don't forget that you're supposed to make an appointment with that new doctor. The card is in your purse."

"I'll do it right away."

He leaned forward and kissed her on the forehead, a soft and lingering brush of his lips, then he turned to leave.

"Ash?"

He turned back. "Yeah?"

"Thank you. For everything. I probably haven't said that enough. I know it's been a rough week, and you've been wonderful."

"I'm just glad to have you home," he said. He flashed her one last sweet smile, then disappeared from sight. Not a minute later she heard the jingle of his car keys, then the sound of the door opening and closing, then silence.

As promised, the first thing she did was fish the doctor's card from her purse and called to make the appointment. It was scheduled for Friday of that week, three days away at nine in the morning. Ash would have to drive her of course, which would mean him taking even more time off work. Maybe he could just drop her off and pick her up. She wondered if it was close to his work. The receptionist spouted off cross streets and directions, none of which Melody recognized, but she dutifully jotted them down for Ash.

With that finished, she stepped back into her bedroom, wondering what she should investigate first. There was a desk and file cabinet on one side of the room, and a chest of drawers on the other. But as her eyes swept over the bed, she was overcome by a yawn so deep that tears welled in her eyes.

Maybe she should rest first, then investigate, she thought, already walking to the bed. She pulled down the covers and slipped between sheets so silky soft she longed to shed all of her clothes, but this was going to be a short rest, not a full-blown nap.

But the second her head hit the pillow she was sound asleep.

Despite how many times Ash reminded himself what Melody had done to him, she was starting to get under his skin. He was sure that going to work, getting back to his old routine, would put things in perspective. Instead, as he rode the elevator up to the sixth floor, his shoulders sagged with the weight of his guilt.

Maybe it was wrong to leave Melody alone so soon. Would it have really been so terrible waiting until tomorrow to return to work? But he'd felt as though he desperately needed time away, if only a few hours, to get her off his mind. Only now that he was gone, he felt so bad for leaving, she was all he could think about.

Damned if he did, damned if he didn't.

The halls were deserted as he stepped off the elevator, but when he entered his outer office his secretary, Rachel, who'd single-handedly held his professional life together this week, jumped from her chair to greet him.

"Mr. Williams! You're back! I thought we wouldn't see you until tomorrow." She walked around her desk to give him a warm hug. He wouldn't ordinarily get physically affectionate with his subordinates, especially a woman. But considering she was pushing sixty and happily married with three kids and half a dozen grandchildren, he wasn't worried. Besides, she was sometimes more of a mother figure than a secretary. She reminded him of his own mother in many ways, of what she might have been like if she'd lived. However, no matter how many times he'd asked, she refused to address him by his first name. She was very old-fashioned that way. She had been with Maddox *long* before he came along, and probably knew more about the business than most of the hotshots working there.

"I decided to come in for a few hours, to catch up on things," he told her.

Rachel backed away, holding him at arm's length. "You look tired."

"And you look gorgeous. Is that a new hairstyle?"

She rolled her eyes at his less-than-subtle dodge. He knew as well as she did that her hair hadn't changed in twenty years. "How is Melody?"

"On the mend. She should be back to her old self in no time."

"I'm so glad to hear that. Send her my best."

"I will." Rachel knew Melody had been in an accident, but not the severity of it, or that she had amnesia. There would be too many questions that Ash just didn't have the answers to.

It was best he kept Melody as far removed from his life as he could, so the inevitable breakup wouldn't cause more than a minor ripple.

When rumors of her leaving the first time had circulated, the compassionate smiles and looks of pity were excruciating. He didn't appreciate everyone sticking their noses in his personal life, when it was no one else's business.

Rachel looked him up and down, one brow raised. "Did someone make it casual day and forget to tell me?"

He chuckled. "Since I'm not officially here, I thought I could get away with it."

"I'll let it slide this one time." She patted his shoulder. "Now, you go sit down. Coffee?"

"That would be fantastic. Thanks." He was so zonked that if he were to put his head down on his desk he would go out like a light. He'd slept terrible last night, knowing that Mel was just a few feet away in the next bed, naked. It only made matters worse that she insisted on walking around the room naked beforehand.

While Rachel fetched his coffee, Ash walked into his office. It was pretty much the way he'd left it, except his inbox had multiplied exponentially in size. He was going to have to stay all weekend playing catch-up. Just as he settled into his chair Rachel returned with his coffee and a pastry.

"I know you prefer to avoid sweets, but you looked as if you could use the sugar."

"Thanks, Rachel." He'd been eating so terribly the past week that one little Danish wasn't going to make much difference. Kind of like throwing a deck chair off the Titanic. Thankfully the hotel in Abilene had had a fitness room, and he'd used it faithfully each morning before he left for the hospital.

"I there anything else?" she asked.

He sipped his coffee and shook his head. "I'm good."

"Buzz if you need me," she said, then left his office, shutting the door behind her.

Ash sighed, gazing around the room, feeling conflicted. He loved his job, and being here usually brought him solace, yet now he felt as if there were somewhere else he should be instead.

With Melody, of course. All the more reason not to go home.

Ash picked up the pastry and took a bite. Someone knocked on his door, then it opened and Flynn stuck his head in.

"I see our wandering CFO had finally returned to the flock. You got a minute?"

Ash's mouth was full so he gestured Flynn in. He swallowed and said, "I'm not officially back until tomorrow, so I'm not really here."

"Gotcha." He made himself comfortable in the chair opposite his desk. "So, after you left so abruptly last week I tried to pump Rachel for information but she clammed up on me. I even threatened to fire her if she didn't talk and she said this place would tank without her."

"It probably would," Ash agreed.

"Which is why she's still sitting out there and I'm in here asking you why you disappeared. I know your parents are dead, and you never mentioned any relatives, so it can't be that. I'm guessing it had something to do with Melody." He paused then said, "Of course you can tell me to go to hell and mind my own business."

He could, and it was tempting, but Ash figured he owed Flynn an explanation. Not only was Flynn his boss, he was a friend. However, he had to be careful to edit the content. Maddox had some very conservative clients. Conservative, *multimillion-dollar* clients. If rumors began to circulate that his mistress of three years left him because she was carrying another man's love-child, it would only be a matter of time before word made it to someone at Golden Gate Promotions, who wouldn't hesitate to use it against Maddox.

Not that he believed Flynn would deliberately do anything to jeopardize the success of the company his own father built from the ground up, but despite the best of intentions, things had a way of slipping out. Like the affair that Brock, Flynn's brother, was rumored to be having with his assistant. Brock and Elle probably never intended that to get out either.

It just wasn't worth the risk.

"I found her," Ash told Flynn.

"You told me you weren't even going to look."

"Yeah, well, after a few weeks, when she didn't come crawling back to me begging forgiveness, I got…concerned. So I hired a P.I."

"So where was she?"

"In a hospital in Abilene, Texas."

His brow dipped low over his eyes. "A hospital? Is she okay?"

Ash told him the whole story. The accident, the drug-induced coma, all the time he spent by her bedside, then having to drive home because she couldn't fly.

Flynn shook his head in disbelief. "I wish you would have said something. Maybe there was a way we could have helped."

"I appreciate it, but really, there was nothing you could have done. She just needs time to heal."

"Is she back home with you now?"

"Yeah, we got back today."

"So, does this mean you guys are…back together?"

"She's staying with me while she recovers. After that…" He shrugged. "We'll just have to wait and see."

"This is probably none of my business, but did she tell you why she left?"

"It's…complicated."

Flynn held up a hand. "I get it, back off. Just know that I'm here if you need to talk. And if you need anything, Ash, anything at all, just say the word. Extra vacation days, a leave of absence, you name it and it's yours. I want to do anything I can to help."

He wouldn't be taking Flynn up on that. The idea of spending another extended amount of time away from work, stuck in his condo, just him and Melody, made his chest feel tight. "Thanks, Flynn, I appreciate it. We both do."

After he was gone Ash sat at his desk replaying the conversation in his head. He hadn't lied to Flynn; he'd just left out a few facts. For Flynn's own good, and the good of the company.

His mom used to tell him that good intentions paved the way to hell, and Ash couldn't escape the feeling sometimes that maybe he was already there.

Eight

Melody's quick rest turned into an all-day affair. She roused at seven-thirty when Ash got back feeling more tired than before, with a blazing headache to boot. After feeling so good the day before, the backslide was discouraging. Ash assured her that it was probably just the lingering aftereffects of the barometer and temperature change going from Texas to California, and she hoped he was right.

She popped two painkillers then joined him at the dining-room table in her sleep-rumpled clothes and nibbled on a slice of the pizza he'd brought home with him. She had hoped they could spend a few hours together, but the pills seemed to hit her especially hard. Despite sleeping most of the day, she could barely hold her head up. At one point she closed her eyes, for what she thought was just a second, but the next thing she knew Ash was nudging her awake.

"Let's get you into bed," he said, and she realized that he had already cleared the table and put the pizza away.

Melody stood with his help and let him lead her to the bedroom. She crawled in bed, clothes and all, and only vaguely recalled feeling him pull the covers up over her and kiss her forehead.

When she woke the next morning she felt a million times better. Her head still hurt, but the pain was mild, and her stomach howled to be fed. Wearing the same clothes as yesterday, her hair a frightening mop that she twisted and fastened in place with a clip she found under the bathroom sink, she wandered out of her bedroom in search of Ash, but he had already left for work.

The coffee in the pot was still warm so she poured herself a cup and put it in the microwave to heat, finding that her fingers seemed to know exactly what buttons to push, even though she had no memory of doing it before. While she waited she fixed herself something to eat. She spent a good forty minutes on the couch, devouring cold pizza, sipping lukewarm coffee and watching an infomercial advertising some murderously uncomfortable looking contraption of spandex and wire that when worn over the bra was designed to enhance the breasts and improve posture. She couldn't imagine ever being so concerned about the perkiness of her boobs that she would subject herself to that kind of torture.

She also wondered, if she'd never gone to Texas, and the accident hadn't happened, what she would be doing right now? Would she be sprawled on the couch eating leftovers or out doing something glamorous like meeting with her personal trainer or getting her legs waxed?

Or would she be in class? It was only mid-April so the semester wouldn't be over yet. She wondered, when and if she got her memory back, if they would let her make up the time and work she'd missed or if she would have to go back and take the classes over again. If she even wanted to go back, that was. The law still held little interest, but that could change. And what if it didn't? What then?

Worrying about it was making her head hurt, so she pushed it out of her mind. She got up, put her dirty dishes in the dishwasher alongside Ash's coffee cup and cereal bowl, then went to take a long, hot shower. She dried off with a soft, oversize, fluffy blue towel, then stood naked in her closet trying to decide what to wear. Much like the bras she had packed for her trip, everything she owned seemed to be a push-up or made of itchy lace—or both. Didn't she own any no-nonsense, comfortable bras?

It gave her the inexplicable feeling that she was rummaging through someone else's wardrobe.

She found a drawer full of sport bras that would do until she could get to the store and put one on. Maybe she'd liked those other bras before, and maybe she would again someday, but for now they just seemed uncomfortable and impractical. The same went for all the thong, lace underwear. Thank goodness she had a few silk and spandex panties, too.

She was so used to lying around in a hospital gown that the designer-label clothes lining her closet seemed excessive when all she planned to do was hang out at home, but after some searching she found a pair of black cotton yoga pants and a Stanford University sweatshirt that had been washed and worn to within an inch of its life.

Since she was already in the closet, she decided that would be the place to start her search for memory-jogging paraphernalia. But around ten, when Ash called to check on her, nothing she'd found held any significance. Just the typical stuff you would find in any woman's closet. She wondered if she was trying too hard. If she stopped thinking about it, maybe it would just come to her. But the thought of sitting around doing nothing seemed totally counterproductive.

Refusing to let herself get frustrated, she searched her desk next. She found papers in her hand that she had no recollection of writing, and an envelope of photos of herself and Ash, most in social settings. She'd hoped maybe there would be letters or a diary but there were none.

In the file cabinet she found pages and pages of school-work and other school-related papers, but nothing having to do with any specific research she'd been working on. In the very back of the drawer she found an unmarked file with several DVDs inside. Most were unmarked, but one had a handwritten label marked *Ash's Birthday*. Video of a birthday party maybe? Home videos could jog a memory, right?

Full of excitement and hope, she grabbed the file and dashed out to the family room to the enormous flat-screen television. It took her a few minutes just to figure out how to turn everything on, and which remote went with which piece of equipment. When the disk was in and loaded she sat on the couch and hit Play...and discovered in the first two seconds that this was no ordinary birthday party. At least, not the kind they would invite other people to. For starters, they were in bed...and in their underwear. Those didn't stay on for long though.

This was obviously one of those videos that Ash had mentioned. Although, at the time, she had half believed he was joking. She felt like a voyeur, peeking through a window at another woman's private life. The things she was doing to him, the words coming out of her mouth, made her blush furiously, but she was too captivated to look away. Was this the kind of thing Ash was going to expect when they made love? Because she wasn't sure if she even knew how to be that woman anymore. She was so blatantly sexy and confident.

Melody hated her for it, and desperately wanted to *be* her.

When the DVD ended she grabbed one of the unmarked DVDs and put it in the player. It was similar to the first one, starting out with the two of them in bed together. But this time after a bit of foreplay she reached over somewhere out of the camera's view, and came back with four crimson silk scarves that she used to tie a very willing Ash to the head and footboard.

Watching this DVD she discovered just how flexible she actually was. Physically and sexually. It was sexy and adventurous, and in a lot of ways fun, but it occurred to her as it ended that she wasn't particularly turned on. More curious than aroused. Not that she didn't enjoy seeing Ash naked. His body was truly a work of art. Long and lean and perfect in every way. It was the sex itself that was, she hated to admit, a little...boring.

She grabbed a third disk and put it in, and as it began to play she could tell right away that it was different. This one was set in Ash's bathroom, and he was filming her through the clear glass shower door. She was soaping herself up, seemingly lost in thought. He said her name, and when she turned she looked genuinely surprised to see him standing there holding the camera. After that he must have put the camera on a tripod because he came from behind it, already beautifully naked, and climbed in the stall with her, leaving the door open.

The tone of this video was completely different from the others. They soaped each other up, touching and stroking, as if they had all the time in the world. And unlike the others there was a lot of kissing in this one. Deep, slow, tender kisses that had Melody's attention transfixed to screen, actually licking her lips, wishing she could taste Ash there.

Missing was the sense of urgency, as if it were a race to see who could get who off first. Instead they took their time exploring and caressing, their arousal gradually escalating, until they both seemed to lose themselves. It was like watching a totally different couple, and this was a woman she could definitely imagine being. A woman she *wanted* to be.

The first two DVDs had been sexy, but they were just sex. There didn't seem to be much emotion involved. In this one it was clear, by the way they touched, the way they looked in each other's eyes, that they had a deep emotional connection. She could *see* that they loved each other.

On the screen Ash lifted her off her feet and pressed her against the shower wall. Their eyes locked and held, and the ecstasy on their faces, the look of total rapture as he sank inside her made Melody shiver.

She *wanted* that. She wanted Ash to kiss her and touch her and make love to her. She was breathing heavily, feeling so warm and tingly between her thighs that she wished she could climb through the screen and take the other Melody's place. They were making love in the purest sense, and she couldn't help thinking that if he were here right now she would—

"This one is my favorite," someone said from behind her.

Melody shrieked in surprise and flew off the couch so fast that the remote went flying and landed with a sharp crack on the hardwood floor several feet away. She spun around and found Ash standing behind the couch, a couple of plastic grocery bags hanging from his fingers and a wry grin on his face.

"You scared me half to death!" she admonished, her

anger a flimsy veil to hide her embarrassment. But it
was useless because her face was already turning twenty
different shades of pink. He'd caught her watching porn.
Porn that *he* was in. What could be more embarrassing?
"You shouldn't sneak up on people."

"I wasn't sneaking. In fact, I wasn't being particularly
quiet at all. You just didn't hear me. I guess I see why."

On the television her evil counterpart was moaning and
panting as Ash rocked into her, water sluicing down their
wet, soapy bodies. Melody scrambled for the remote, but
it took her a few seconds of jabbing random buttons before
the DVD stopped and the screen went black. When she
looked back at Ash he was still wearing that wry smile.

"What are you doing home? It's only—" she looked
at the clock and could hardly believe it was after three
"—three-fifteen."

Had she really been watching sex videos for almost two
hours?

He held up the bags. "There's nothing here to eat but
pizza so I stopped at the store after a lunch meeting. So
you wouldn't have to go out."

"Oh. Thank you."

She waited for a comment about her watching the video,
waited for him to tease her, but instead he walked past her
and carried the bags to the kitchen. It was the first time she
had seen him in a suit since the day he showed up at the
hospital to claim her, and, oh, man, did he look delicious.
There was something undeniably sexy about an executive
who shopped for groceries. Of course, as turned on as she
was right now, he would look sexy in plaid polyester floods
and a polka-dot argyle sweater.

"I found the DVDs in my file cabinet," she said,
following him, even though he hadn't asked for an

explanation, or even looked as though he expected or required one.

He set the bags on the island countertop and started unpacking them. It looked as though he had picked up the basics. Milk, eggs, bread, a gallon of orange juice, as well as two bags full of fresh fruits and vegetables.

"I didn't know what they were when I found them," she said, stepping around to put the perishables in the fridge. "I was pretty surprised when I put the first one in."

One brow rose. "The *first* one?"

God, she made it sound as if she had been sitting there watching them all day.

"The *only* one," she lied, but it was obvious he wasn't buying it. Probably because he'd seen the DVDs strewn out on the coffee table.

"Okay, maybe I watched two…"

Up the brow went again.

"…and a *half.* It would have been three if I'd finished the one I was watching when you walked in."

He seemed to find her discomfort amusing. "Mel, watch as many as you like."

She wondered if he really meant that. "It doesn't… *bother* you?"

"Why would it?" he asked, looking very *un*bothered.

"Because you're in them, and they're very… personal."

He gave her a weird look. "You're in them, too."

"Yeah, but…it doesn't *seem* like me. It's like I'm watching someone else do all those things."

"Take my word for it, it was definitely you." He emptied the last of the bags so she balled them up, shoving one inside the other, and tossed them in the recycling bin under the sink.

"So," she said, turning to him. "The shower one is your favorite?"

He grinned and nodded, and she wondered if she could talk him into re-creating it someday soon. It only seemed fair, seeing as how she could no longer remember doing it.

"It was mine, too," she said.

"Why do you suppose that is?"

"I guess because it seemed more...*real*."

That brow rose again. "Are you suggesting that in the others you were faking it?"

"No! Of course not," she said, but realized, maybe she had been. The first two had been lacking something. They seemed almost...*staged*. As if she had been putting on a show for the camera. And there was no denying that, now at least, the hot sex and dirty talk didn't do half as much for her as watching them make love.

Had she been faking it in those first two?

"You look as though you're working something through," Ash said. He was standing with his arms folded, hip wedged against the counter. He narrowed his eyes at her. "*Were* you faking it?"

She hoped not. What was the point of even having sex if she wasn't going to enjoy it? "Even if I was, I wouldn't remember. Would I?"

"That's awfully convenient."

She frowned. "No. It isn't. Not for me."

"Sorry." He reached out and touched her arm. "I didn't mean it like that."

She knew that. He was only teasing and she was being too touchy. She forced a smile. "I know you didn't. Don't worry about it." She grabbed the last of the items on the counter, opened the pantry and put them away.

Ask looked at his watch. "Damn, it's getting late, I have

to get back. Thanks for helping put away—" He frowned and said, "Wait a minute."

He walked to the fridge and opened it, scanning the inside, all the drawers and compartments, as if he'd forgotten something, then he closed the refrigerator door and looked in the cabinet under the kitchen sink. He did the same thing to the pantry, then he turned to her and asked, "Do you realize what you just did?"

Considering the look on his face, it couldn't have been good. "No. Did I put everything in the wrong place or something?"

"No. Mel, you put everything in the *right* place."

"I did?" She wanted to believe it was significant, but at the same time she didn't want to get her hopes up. "Maybe it was a coincidence?"

"I don't think so. When it comes to your kitchen you're almost fanatical about keeping things tidy and organized. Everything in there is on the correct shelf, or in the right drawer. You even put the bags in the recycling bin when we were done and I don't recall telling you it was even there."

He was right. She hadn't even thought about putting them there, she just did it. Just like the law stuff. It just came to her naturally, by doing and not thinking.

Her heart started to beat faster and happiness welled up, putting a huge lump in her throat. "You think I'm remembering?"

"I think you are."

She squealed and threw herself into his arms, hugging him tight, feeling so happy she could burst. She realized, especially after watching those DVDs, just how many things she *wanted* to remember.

She laid her head on his shoulder and closed her eyes, breathing in the scent of his aftershave. It felt so good to be close to him. Even if he wasn't hugging her back as hard as she was hugging him. "Do you think it was the DVDs? Maybe watching them made me remember the other things?"

"Maybe."

She smiled up at him. "Well, then, maybe the real thing would work even better."

He got that stern look and she quickly backpedaled. "I know, I know. I'm not ready. Yet. It was just…an observation. For when I *am* ready." Which she was thinking might be sooner than they both expected.

He smoothed her hair back from her face and pressed a kiss to her forehead. "I think, when your brain is ready to remember things, it will. I don't think you can rush it. Every time you've remembered something it's been when you weren't thinking about it. Right?"

She nodded.

"So just relax and let it happen naturally." He looked at his watch, gave her one last kiss on the forehead, and said, "Now I really have to go."

She was disappointed, but didn't let it show. "Thanks for bringing the groceries. I suppose I should think about making something for dinner."

"Don't worry about feeding me. I'll probably be home late. I have a lot of work to catch up on."

Which was her fault, so she couldn't exactly complain. She walked him to the elevator instead, watching until he stepped inside and the doors closed.

This time it was definitely not her imagination. Knowing that she was remembering things troubled him for some reason, and the only reason she could come up with was that there was something that he didn't *want* her to remember. But she had no clue why, or what it could be. She thought about the money that she'd stashed in the pocket of one of the jackets in her closet. Was that the key to all of this?

She decided that if she had any more epiphanies or memory breakthroughs it would be best, for the time being anyway, to keep them to herself.

Nine

Ash took Friday morning off so he could take Mel to her appointment with her new neurologist. She had offered to have Ash drop her off and pick her up when she was finished, so he wouldn't miss more work, but the truth was he wanted to be there to hear what the doctor had to say.

It had been eerie the other day, watching her put the groceries away, only to realize that, right before his eyes, she was becoming herself again. She was remembering, no matter how small and insignificant a memory it had been. The point was, it was happening, and he wasn't sure he was ready.

Although since then, she hadn't mentioned remembering anything new. Not that he'd been around to witness it himself. Work had kept him at the office until almost midnight the past three days so he and Mel had barely seen each other.

The doctor gave her a thorough neurological exam,

asked a couple dozen questions, and seemed impressed by her progress. He suggested that she slowly begin adding more physical activities back to her daily regimen. Mel glanced over at Ash, and he knew exactly the sort of *physical activities* she was thinking of. And he knew, the second she opened her mouth, what she was going to say.

"What about sex?" she asked.

The doctor looked down at the chart, a slight frown crinkling his brow, and for one terrifying instant Ash thought he was going to mention the miscarriage. Had Dr. Nelson warned him not to say anything? Finding out about the baby now would ruin everything.

"I see no reason why you shouldn't engage in sexual activity," he said, then added with a smile. "I would caution against anything too vigorous at first. Just take it slow and do what you're comfortable with. I also suggest walking."

"I've been doing that. We live right by the water so I've been taking walks on the shore."

"That's good. Just don't overdo it. Start at ten or fifteen minutes a day and gradually work your way up." He closed her file. "Well, everything looks good. If you have any problems, call me. Otherwise, I won't need to see you back for three months."

"That's it?" Mel asked. "We're really done?"

The doctor smiled. "At this point there isn't much I can do. But only because Dr. Nelson took very good care of you."

He shook hers and then Ash's hand, and then he left. From the time they stepped into the waiting room, the entire appointment hadn't taken more than twenty minutes.

"That sure was quick," Mel said as they walked to

the reception desk to make her next appointment. "I was expecting CAT scans and EEGs and all sorts of tests. I'd thought I'd be trapped here all day."

So had he. Now that it was out of the way he was anxious to get back to work.

He drove her home and went up with her to grab his briefcase. He planned to say a quick goodbye and head out, but he could see by her expression that she wanted to "talk" and he knew exactly what about. Honestly, he was surprised she hadn't brought it up the second they got out of the doctor's office.

"Okay, let's have it," he said, dropping his briefcase beside the couch and perching on the arm.

She smiled shyly, which was weird because Mel didn't have a shy bone in her body. Or didn't used to. He couldn't deny that he liked it a little. "So, you heard what the doctor said, about it being okay to make love."

"When you're ready," he added, hoping she didn't think they were going to throw down right here on the living-room rug. Not that he hadn't been thinking about it either, after walking in to find her watching their home movies.

She had been so transfixed by the image of the two of them in the shower that she hadn't heard him come in. He'd taken his keys from the lock and gave them an extra jingle to alert her to his presence. When that didn't work he'd shut the door with more force than necessary, but she hadn't even flinched. He'd tried rustling the plastic bags he was holding, and determined at that point that it was a lost cause. She had been so captivated, it was as if the rest of the world had ceased to exist. Then he'd stepped closer to the couch, seen the rapid rise and fall of her chest as she breathed, the blush of arousal in her cheeks. She'd clenched the edge of the couch, looking as though she were about to climb out of her own skin.

The last time he'd seen her that turned on was when they had made that DVD.

In that instant he knew he wanted her, and it was just a matter of time before he gave in and let her have her way with him. But he'd wanted to wait and make sure everything went all right with her doctor appointment. And now he'd been given a green light.

When she didn't say anything, he asked, "Do you feel like you're ready?"

She shrugged. "I don't know. I guess I won't be sure until I try."

He waited for her to suggest that they try right now, but she didn't. Instead she asked, "Are you working late again?"

"Until at least nine," he said. "Probably later."

She sighed. "I'll be really happy when you're caught up and we can actually see each other for more than ten minutes in the morning before you walk out the door. And maybe one of these days I'll actually get to make dinner for you."

"Soon," he said, not sure if that was a promise he could, or *wanted*, to keep. He needed to keep some distance between them.

He waited for her to bring up the subject of sex again, but surprisingly, she didn't. "Anything else before I go?" he asked.

She shook her head. "I don't think so."

Oookay. With affirmation from the doctor, he expected her to all but throw herself at him. Why was she acting so...timid?

He walked to the door and she followed him. "Call me later and I'll try to wait up for you," she said.

"I will." He leaned down to brush a kiss to her cheek, but this time she turned her head and it was her lips he touched instead. He had kissed Mel at least a million times before, but this time when their lips met he felt it like an electric charge. Her sudden sharp intake of breath told him that she'd felt it, too. They stood that way for several seconds, frozen, their lips barely touching. He waited for her to make her move, but after several seconds passed and she didn't move, didn't even breathe as far as he could tell, he took matters into his own hands. He leaned in first, pressing his lips to hers.

Her lips were warm and soft and familiar and she still tasted like toothpaste. He waited for her to launch herself at him, to dive in with her usual enthusiasm, to ravage him with the deep, searching, desperate kisses that sometimes made him feel as though she wanted to swallow him whole.

But she didn't. In fact it took several seconds before he felt her lips part, and she did it hesitantly, as if she was afraid to push too far too fast. Even when their tongues touched it wasn't more than a tentative taste.

He'd never kissed her this way before, so tender and sweet. She didn't dive in with gusto, in what he had to admit sometimes felt more like an oral assault than a kiss. Not that it wasn't hot as hell, but this was nice, too. In fact, he liked this a lot.

It was so different, so *not* Melody. Even though he'd sworn to himself that he'd take this slow, he let himself be drawn in. Let her drag him down into something warm and sexy and satisfying.

He realized something else was different, too. Melody always wore perfume or body spray. The same musky, sensual fragrance that at times could be a touch cloying. Now the only detectable scent was a hint of soap and shampoo intermingled with the natural essence of her skin and her hair. Honestly, it was sexier and more arousing than anything she could find in a bottle.

And he was aroused, he realized. He was erect to the point of discomfort and aching for release. If her labored breathing and soft whimpers were any indication, he wouldn't have to wait long.

He deepened the kiss and her tongue tangled with his, and she tasted so delicious, felt so good melting against him, he was the one who wanted to ravish her. He had promised himself that he would make her wait a little longer, draw out the anticipation for another day or two, until he really had her crawling out of her skin, but at that precise moment, he didn't give a damn what he'd promised himself. He wanted her *now*.

Just as he was ready to make the next move, take it to the next level, he felt Mel's hands on his chest applying gentle but steady pressure, and he realized that she was pushing him away.

He broke the kiss and reluctantly backed off. "What's wrong?"

Melody's cheeks were deep red and he could see her pulse fluttering wildly at the base of her neck. She smiled up at him and said, a little breathlessly, "That was amazing. But I think it's all I can handle right now."

All she could *handle?* Was she kidding? Once Mel got started she was unstoppable. Now she was actually stopping him?

Ash was so stunned by her sudden change of heart that he wasn't sure how to act or what to say to her. She had never told him no. In fact, since he met her, he couldn't recall a time when he'd even had to *ask* for sex. She was usually the aggressor, and she had an insatiable appetite. There were even times when he wished they could take a day or two off.

Now, for the first time in three years, he wanted something that he couldn't have.

It was a sobering realization.

"I'm sorry," she said, and he realized she was gazing up at him, looking apologetic. "I just don't want to rush things. I want to take it slow, just like you said."

For a second he had to wonder if this was some sort of twisted game. Get him all hot and bothered then say no. But the thought was fleeting because the Melody gazing up at him wasn't capable of that kind of behavior. He was the one who had all but scolded her for touching him in the hotel room, the one who kept saying that they should take it slowly.

If anyone was playing games, he was, and he was getting exactly what he deserved.

"Are you okay?" she asked, her mouth pulled into a frown. "Are you upset with me?"

He desperately wished she was the old Melody again, so he could use this opportunity to hurt her. But in his mind they had inexplicably split into two separate and distinct people. The good Mel, and the evil Mel. And he knew that he couldn't hurt this Melody.

Jesus, he was whipped. He'd gone and let her get under his skin. The *one* thing he swore he wouldn't do.

"No," he said, pulling her into his arms and holding her. "I'm not upset. Not at all."

May as well enjoy it while it lasted, he thought, as she snuggled against him, burying her face in the crook of his neck. He knew, with her memory slowly returning, it was only a matter of time before the evil Mel was back and the good Mel was lost forever.

It was inevitable, but damn, was he going to miss her.

Leaving Mel and going in to work had been tough, but not as tough as it would have been staying with her. Sex had been the furthest thing from his mind the past couple weeks, but now, after one damned kiss, it seemed it was all he could think about. As a result, he was having one hell of a time concentrating on work.

He took an early lunch, early being noon instead of two or three, and though he didn't normally drink during work hours, he made an exception and ordered a scotch on the rocks. It helped a little.

On his way back to his office he ran into Brock Maddox.

"I was just going to call you," Brock said. "Can I have a quick word?"

"Of course."

He gestured Ash to his office, and when they were inside he closed the door and said, "Flynn told me what happened with Melody. I wanted you to know how sorry I am."

"Thanks. But she's actually doing really well. She had an appointment with her neurologist today and everything looks good."

"I'm relieved to hear it."

"Was that all?" Ash asked, moving toward the door.

"There's one more thing. As you've probably heard, we didn't get the Brady account."

"I heard." Brady Enterprises was a fairly large account, and the fact that they didn't get it was unfortunate, but Ash wasn't sure if it warranted the grim look Brock was wearing. As CFO, Ash knew they were financially sound with or without Brady.

"They hired Golden Gate Promotions," Brock told him.

"I heard that, too." It was never fun to lose, especially to a direct competitor, especially one as cocky and arrogant as Athos Koteas, but obviously Golden Gate pitched them an idea, and a budget, they couldn't refuse.

"Did you hear that they low-balled us out of the deal?" Brock asked, and when Ash opened his mouth to respond, he added, "Using a pitch that was almost identical to ours."

"What?"

"That's more the reaction I was hoping for."

"Where did you hear this?"

"I have an acquaintance over at Brady and she clued me in. She said it was even suggested that Maddox was stealing pitch ideas."

"Are we?"

The question seemed to surprise Brock. "Hell, no! That was *our* idea."

"So, how did Golden Gate manage to pitch the same thing? Coincidence?"

"Highly unlikely. The only explanation is that someone here leaked it."

If that was true, they had a serious problem. "What does Flynn think of this?"

"I didn't tell him yet."

As vice president, Flynn should have been told about this immediately. "You don't think he needs to know?"

"I wanted to talk to you first."

"Why? As CFO, this really isn't my area of expertise."

"Look, Ash, I'm not sure how to say this, so I'm just going to say it. You know that I've always liked Melody, but is it possible that she could have had anything to do with this?"

The question was so jarring, so out-of-the-blue unexpected, it actually knocked Ash back a step or two. *"Melody?* What would she have to do with this?"

"It just seems coincidental that right around the time we started laying out the framework for the pitch, meetings you were in on, she disappeared. I would understand completely if maybe you went home and mentioned things to her, never suspecting that she would leak it to our competitor. Maybe they made her an offer she couldn't refuse."

Ash's hands curled into fists at his sides, and had he been standing within arm's reach, he might have actually slugged Brock. "The idea that you would accuse Melody of all people of corporate espionage is the most ridiculous, not to mention *insulting,* thing I've ever heard."

"Considering the way she took off, it just seemed a plausible scenario."

"Yeah, well, you are *way* off base," Ash said, taking a step toward him, all but daring him to disagree.

Brock put his hands up in a defensive posture and said, "Whoa, take it easy, Ash. I apologize for offending you, but put yourself in my position for a minute. Like I said, I *had* to ask. There's a rumor that she didn't leave on the best of terms, so I figured—"

"So we're listening to rumors now? So should I assume that you're screwing your assistant?"

Brock's brow dipped in anger and Ash had the distinct feeling he'd taken this argument a step too far, then Brock's attention shifted to the door.

"Mother, would it really be too much for you to knock before you enter a room?"

Ash turned to see Carol Maddox standing in the now-open doorway. Small and emaciated but a force to be reckoned with nonetheless. And oh, man, she didn't look pleased. Of course, as long as Ash had known her, disappointment and contempt were the only two expressions that had ever made it through the Botox. In fact, he couldn't recall a single incidence when he'd seen her smile. She was probably one of the unhappiest, nastiest people he'd ever met, and seemed hell-bent on taking everyone else down with her.

"I need to have a word with you, dear," she said through gritted teeth, or maybe the Botox had frozen her jaw. Either way, she looked royally pissed off and Ash was in no mood to get caught in the crosshairs.

"I take it we're finished here," he said, and Brock nodded curtly.

As Ash sidestepped around Mrs. Maddox to get to the door, he almost felt guilty. The remark about Brock sleeping with Elle didn't seem to go over well with good ol' mom. But that was what he got for accusing Melody of all people of leaking company secrets.

Even if Ash had told her about the campaign—which he definitely hadn't—she was not the type to go selling the information to Maddox's rival. And somewhere deep down he would always resent Brock for even suggesting that she would.

Wait a minute…

He gave himself a mental shake. Wasn't he being a touch hypocritical? Why was he so dead set on defending the honor of a woman he planned to use, then viciously dump? This was the evil Mel they were talking about, right?

Because, although she may have betrayed Ash's trust, it would be against everything he believed to castigate someone for something they didn't do. And for this, she was completely innocent.

When he reached his office Rachel greeted him anxiously. "Oh, *there* you are. I've been calling you. Miss Trent called."

"Sorry, I forgot my cell in my desk. What did she want?"

"She said she needed to talk to you and she sounded frantic. *Completely* unlike herself. She asked to have you call her immediately on her cell phone."

Melody *wasn't* the frantic type, and that alone alarmed him. "Did she say why?"

"No. But I'm worried. She acted as if she'd never spoken to me before."

That was because, as far as she knew, she never had. "I'll call her right away."

He stepped into his office, shut the door and dialed her cell. She answered before it even had time to ring on his end, and the stark fear in her voice made his heart drop.

"Ash?"

"It's me. What's wrong?"

"I need you to come get me," she said, her voice quivering so hard he could barely understand her. His first thought was that maybe something had happened and she needed to be taken to the hospital.

"Are you hurt? Did you hit your head?"

"No, I just need a ride," she said, then he heard the sound of traffic in the background and realized that she must not be at home. She'd said something about taking a walk when he left for work. Had she maybe walked too far and couldn't make it back on her own?

"Mel, where are you?"

"The Hyde Street Pier."

The Hyde Street Pier? That was *way* the hell across town from their condo. There was no way she could have walked that far. "How did you get over there?"

"Can you just come?" she asked, sounding desperate.

"Of course. I'm leaving right now. I'm ten minutes away."

"I'll be in front of the Maritime store right on the corner."

Ash hung up the phone, grabbed his keys from his desk drawer, and as he passed Rachel's desk he said, "I have to run out for a while. I'll try to make it back this afternoon."

"Is everything okay?" she asked, looking concerned.

"I'm not sure." But he was about to find out.

Ten

Melody didn't have to remember her past to know that she had never felt so stupid or humiliated in her *entire* life.

She sat in the passenger seat of Ash's car, wringing her hands in her lap, wishing she could make herself invisible. At least she'd stopped trembling, and now that her heart rate had slowed her head had stopped hurting, and she wasn't dizzy anymore either. That didn't stop her from feeling like a total idiot.

"Are you ready to tell me what happened?" Ash asked gently, looking away from the road for a second to slide her a sideways glance.

"You're going to think I'm stupid," she said.

"I won't think you're stupid." He reached over and pried one hand free and curled it under his. "I'm just glad you're okay. You scared me."

She bit her lip.

"Come on, Mel."

"I got lost," she said quickly, immediately wishing she could take it back. But he didn't chastise or make fun of her, not that she thought he would. It didn't make her feel any less like a dope though. And to his credit, he sat there silently waiting for her to elaborate, not pushing at all.

"Remember I said I was going to take a walk?"

He nodded.

"Well, I felt so good, so full of energy, I guess I overestimated my endurance a bit. I got about a mile and a half from home—"

"A mile and a half?" His eyes went wide. *"Mel!"*

"I know, but it felt so good to be in the fresh air, and it was mostly downhill. But then I started to get *really* tired, and the way back was all *up*hill. I knew I wouldn't be able to make it back, so I got on a bus."

"You knew which bus to take?"

"I thought I did. Unfortunately it was the wrong bus. It took me in the opposite direction of home, and by the time I figured it out I was *really* far. So I got off at the next stop and got on a different bus, but that one was going the wrong direction, too. It was such a strange sensation, like I knew deep down that I should know which bus to take, but I kept picking the wrong one."

"Why didn't you ask someone for help?"

"I was too embarrassed. Besides, I felt like I needed to do it on my own."

"And they say men never ask for directions," he said, rolling his eyes, and she couldn't help but crack a smile.

"I rode around for a couple of hours," she continued, "and finally got off at the pier. I had absolutely no idea where I was. I could have been in China for all I knew. Nothing looked familiar. And I guess...I guess I just freaked out. My heart was racing and I had this tightness in my chest, like I was having a heart attack. Then my hands started going numb and I felt like I was going to pass out and that *really* scared me. That's when I called you."

"It sounds like you had a panic attack. I used to get the same thing when I was a kid, when I went in for my treatments."

"Treatments?" she asked.

He paused for a second, then said, "Radiation."

She frowned. "Radiation? What for?"

"Osteosarcoma," he said, then glanced over and added, "Bone cancer."

He had cancer? She'd had no idea. Well, she probably *did*, she just didn't remember. "I know I've probably asked you this before, but when?"

"I was twelve."

"Where was it?"

"My femur."

"How long were you—"

"Not long. Eight months, give or take. They caught it early at my annual physical. A round of radiation and chemo and I was fine."

She was pretty sure it hadn't been as simple as he made it sound. Especially if he had been having panic attacks. "Do you worry... I mean, could it...come back?"

"If it was going to come back it would have a long time ago." He glanced over at her. "If you're worried I'm going to get sick and die on you, I'm probably more likely to be hit by a bus."

"I didn't mean that. I just...I don't know what I meant. The question just popped out. I'm sorry."

He squeezed her hand. "It's okay."

She could see that it was a touchy subject and she didn't want to push it. She just hoped he didn't think that it would ever stop her from marrying him. She was in this for the long haul, until death do them part and all that. And speaking of marriage...

"I was wondering," she said. "Is there a reason you wouldn't tell people at work that we're engaged?"

His shot a glance her way. "Why do you ask?"

"Well, when I called your office, and your secretary asked who it was, I said Ash's fiancée, and she sounded really confused."

"What did she say?"

"She said, *Ash's what?* and I said, *Ash's fiancée, Melody*. I got the distinct impression that she had no idea we were engaged."

"We just haven't officially announced it," he said. "I asked right before you left on your trip, then you didn't come back...." He shrugged.

"So you didn't say anything to anyone."

"It was the last thing on my mind."

"Well, I guess that explains the pictures and the videos."

"What about them?"

"I noticed that I wasn't wearing my engagement ring in a single one. So now I know why."

Melody looked over at him and Ash had a strange look on his face, as if he felt sick to his stomach or something.

"Is it okay that I said something to her? I mean, we have no reason not to announce it now. Right?"

"I've just been so swamped since we've been back, with everything at work, and the doctor's office. The truth is, it completely slipped my mind."

"But it is okay."

He smiled and squeezed her hand again. "Of course."

"Oh, good," she said, feeling relieved. "Since I kind of

already did. To your secretary anyway. Do you think we should plan some sort of engagement party? Or at least call the wedding planner?"

"I think you shouldn't worry about it until you've had more time to heal. There's no rush. Look at what happened today when you got too stressed."

He was right. She knew he was. It was just that she felt this need to get on with her life. This deep-seated urgency to move forward.

Give it time, she told herself. *Eventually you'll be yourself again.*

When they got back to their building, instead of pulling into the underground lot he stopped at the front entrance.

"You have your key?" he asked.

She pulled it from her jacket pocket and jingled it in front of him. "You're not coming up?"

"I really need to get back. You're okay now, right?"

Sort of, but she wasn't exactly looking forward to being alone. But she couldn't be selfish. "I'm okay. Maybe I'll take a nap."

"I'll call you later." He leaned over and kissed her, but not on the cheek or forehead. This time he went straight for her lips. He brushed them softly with his, and she could swear her already shaky knees went a little bit weaker.

"I'll see you later." She got out and shut the door and watched him zip down the block and around the corner. Incidentally, she didn't see him later. Well, not for more than a few seconds when he roused her with a kiss and said good-night.

From the light in the hallway she could see that he was still in his suit, and he had that fresh-from-the-office smell clinging to his clothes, so she knew he had just gotten home. She peered at the clock and saw that it was after midnight.

At least tomorrow was Saturday. They could finally spend some quality time together. Maybe they could take a walk down by the water and have a picnic lunch at the park. She wondered if they had ever done that before. She drifted off to sleep making plans, and woke at eight feeling excited.

She got dressed and as she brushed her teeth she caught the distinct aroma of coffee. She had hoped to be up first, so she could surprise him with breakfast in bed. Looked as though he didn't sleep in on the weekends.

She expected to find him in the kitchen reading the financial section, but he wasn't there. He wasn't in his bedroom either. Where had he gone?

She grabbed her cell off the counter and dialed his cell. He answered on the third ring. "Where are you?" she asked.

"Just pulling into the lot at work. I thought I would get an early start."

"It's Saturday."

"And your point is?"

"I just…I thought we could spend some time together today."

"You know I have a lot of catching up to do."

"What about tomorrow?"

"Working."

He was working on *Sunday?*

Or was he? What if all these late nights and weekends, he was actually somewhere else?

"Ash…are you having an affair?" The words jumped out before she could stop them, and the second they did she wished them back.

And Ash responded just as she would have expected.

Bitterly. "That's really something coming from…" He suddenly went dead silent, and for a second she thought the call had cut out.

"Ash, are you there?"

"Yes, I'm here, and no, I'm not having an affair. I would *never* do that to you."

"I know. I'm sorry for even suggesting it. I'm just… I guess I'm feeling insecure, and lonely. I never see you."

"I missed more than a week of work."

Which was her fault, so she shouldn't complain. That was more or less what he was saying. "I know. You know what, forget I said anything."

"Tell you what, I'll try to make it home in time for dinner tonight, okay?"

"That would be nice."

"I'll call you later and let you know for sure."

"Okay. I—I love you, Ash."

There was a sight pause, then he said, "Me, too. Talk to you later."

She disconnected, feeling conflicted, asking herself the obvious question. *Me, too?* Given the situation, wouldn't the more appropriate response be, *I love you, too?* Shouldn't he be happy that, despite technically knowing him only a couple of weeks, she knew she loved him? Or maybe he thought she was just saying it because she was supposed to. Maybe that was his way of letting her know that it was okay not to say it if she wasn't ready.

Or maybe she was just losing her mind.

She groaned and dropped her forehead against the cool granite countertop, which she realized was a really dumb move when her head began to throb.

Maybe the problem was that she just needed a purpose outside of Ash. She needed to get back to her education, back to law school. She needed a life. Maybe then she wouldn't care how little time Ash had for her.

If he really needed to be at work, why did Ash feel like such a jackass?

Mel was just going to have to learn that this was the way things were. The way it had *always* been. They had always led very separate lives. She was there when he had time for her, and when he didn't she filled her days with school and shopping. And she had never had a problem with that before.

It made sense that being stuck at home would drive her a little nuts. What she needed was a car, and her credit cards back. That should make her happy.

He rode the elevator up to his floor, feeling better about the whole situation, and wasn't surprised to see Rachel sitting there as he approached his office. She always worked half a day on Saturdays. Sometimes longer if there was a critical pitch in the works.

"G'morning, beautiful," he said and she just rolled her eyes.

"Coffee?"

"Please."

He shrugged out of his jacket and had settled behind his desk by the time she returned.

"How is Melody today?" she asked, setting his coffee in front of him.

"Better." He'd given her a very vague explanation of yesterday's event. He said only that she was out, and wasn't feeling well, and didn't think she could get back home on her own. Rachel hadn't said a word to him about his and Melody's supposed engagement. He didn't doubt that she was simply biding her time.

"I'm a little surprised to see you here," she said.

"Why? I always work Saturday."

"Well, with Melody still recovering…"

"She's okay. It's good for her to do things on her own."

Rachel shrugged and said, "If you say so." And before he could tell her to mind her own business she was gone.

Melody was a big girl, and she had always been extremely independent. Once she had a car, and money to spend, she would stop giving him a hard time.

Instead of working he spent the better part of the morning on the phone with his regular car dealership, negotiating a deal. Because he was a regular and valued customer the salesman even offered to bring the model he was interested in over for a test drive. Unfortunately they didn't have one in stock with all the options he wanted and had to ship it in from a dealership in L.A., but delivery was promised on Monday.

With that taken care of, he called to reinstate all the credit cards he'd cancelled when she left. With expedited delivery they would arrive around the same time as the car. By the time Rachel popped in at noon to let him know she was leaving, he was finally ready to start working.

"Stay home tomorrow," Rachel told him. "Melody needs you just as much as these clowns do. Probably more."

"Thanks, Dr. Phil."

She rolled her eyes and walked out.

Not ten minutes later Brock rang him.

"I need you in the conference room now," he said sternly. Considering his tone, this wasn't going to be a friendly chat, and Ash was not in the mood to get chewed out again. He couldn't even imagine what he'd done. Had Brock found something else to pin on Melody?

Dragging himself up from his desk, he headed down

the hall. The normally clear glass walls of the conference room were opaque, which in itself was not a good sign.

The door was closed, so he knocked.

"Come in," Brock snapped.

Jesus, he so didn't need this today. Ash sighed and pushed the door open, ready to tell Brock to go screw himself, and was nearly knocked backward by a roomful of people shouting, "Surprise!" at the top of their lungs.

He must have looked the part because after a beat, everyone started to laugh. They were obviously celebrating something, but he had no idea what. Had he gotten a raise that no one told him about?

On the conference table was a cake, then he noticed the hand-drawn banner draped from the ceiling.

Congratulations, Mr. Melody Trent.

Eleven

People started milling over to Ash, shaking his hand and congratulating him on his engagement. Brock and Flynn and Jason Reagert. Gavin Spencer, Celia Taylor and Celia's fiancé, Evan Reese. There were even a few public relations people, several creatives and a large group of his financial people from the fifth floor.

Everyone knew.

Dammit. So much for it not being a big stink when he dumped Melody.

Between handshakes someone stuck a drink in his hand and he took a long swallow. "You guys really didn't have to do this," he said.

"When we heard the news we knew we had to have some sort of celebration," Flynn said. "We wanted to invite Melody, but Rachel didn't think she would be feeling up to it."

Jesus, what a nightmare that would have been.

Rachel, the person he assumed was responsible for this fiasco, was on the opposite side of the room so it took him a few minutes to make his way over. When he did, she gave him a huge smile and hugged him. "Congratulations, Mr. Williams."

"You are so fired," he said, hugging her back.

She knew it was an empty threat, so she just patted his arm and said, "You're welcome."

Celia approached and handed him another drink. "I figured you could use it. I know you hate big productions like this."

"Thank you." He accepted the glass and took a long drink.

"I can't tell you how thrilled I am for the two of you," she said. "I know how hard the past couple of months have been. I'm so glad everything worked out. Have you set a date?"

He took another slug of his drink. "Not yet."

"I hope you're not planning to elope, or get hitched in Vegas. You know everyone here is expecting an invitation."

Well, then, everyone here was going to be very disappointed.

He finished his drink and someone gave him another, then someone else handed him a slice of cake. As desperately as he wanted to get the hell out of there, he was more or less stuck until the party wound down around three. And though he could have easily drunk himself into a stupor, he stopped at five scotches—although two were doubles. He wasn't drunk by any means, but tipsy enough to know he shouldn't be driving.

When everyone but the executives had cleared out, Ash figured it was finally safe to get the hell out of there. He hadn't gotten squat done. Not work anyway, and he was in no condition to go back to his office.

"I'm going to call a cab and head home," he told everyone.

"We're heading out, too," Celia said. "Why don't you let us drive you? You don't mind, do you, Evan?"

Her fiancé shrugged. "Fine with me. If you want, Celia could take you home in your car and I can follow. That way you won't have to take a cab into work."

"That would be great," Ash said.

Feeling pleasantly buzzed, he said his goodbyes to everyone else, and the three of them headed down to the parking garage.

When he and Celia were alone in the car and on their way to his condo she told him, "There's something we need to talk about."

"Is something wrong?"

"No. Everything is actually going great. But it's clear that the long-distance relationship Evan and I have is going to get tedious."

"But things are okay with you two?"

"Yeah. Things are so good, I'm moving to Seattle at the end of the year."

Ash hated to see her go, but he wasn't exactly surprised. She had fallen pretty hard for Evan. He just wanted her to be happy. "I guess this means you're leaving Maddox?"

"Technically, no. I'll be handling all of the advertising for Reese Enterprises as a consultant for Maddox. I'll just be doing it from Seattle."

"Wow, that's great."

"I told Brock and Flynn I was thinking of leaving, and they didn't want to lose me."

"That's because you've made them a lot of money. They know a good thing when they see it."

"I'm excited, but I'm going to miss everyone here."

"Who's going to take your place?"

"His name is Logan Emerson, he's going to start working with me Monday. I'll train him for a couple of weeks, then I'll be exclusively on the Reese account. I'm sure I'll be doing a lot of traveling back and forth until I make the move."

"Well, we'll miss you, but it sounds like an awesome opportunity."

They reached Ash's building and he directed her down into the parking garage, then they walked up to the street where Evan was waiting.

"Thanks for the ride," he said.

Celia smiled. "No problem. See you Monday. And say congratulations to Melody for us. We should all get together for dinner sometime, when she's feeling better."

"Definitely," he said, knowing that would never happen.

Ash waved as they drove off, then he went upstairs. The condo was quiet so he figured Mel was probably out for a walk, but then he saw her key on the counter. He walked to her room and looked in but she wasn't in bed, then he heard water turn on in her bathroom. He crossed the room, and since the bathroom door was open, he looked in.

Hot damn. Melody was in the shower.

He wondered if she might be in the mood for company. After watching her watch that video the other day, he had the feeling it could get very interesting.

He shrugged out of his jacket and tossed it on the bed, then kicked off his shoes.

He stepped into the bathroom, not being particularly stealthy, but Mel was rinsing shampoo from her hair so her head was thrown back and her eyes were closed. Suds ran down her back and the curve of her behind, and all he could think about was soaping up his hands and rubbing them all over her.

He waited for her to open her eyes, so she would see him there, but when she finally did she turned with her back to him. She grabbed a bottle of soap and poured some out into her hand then turned away from the spray and began soaping herself up. He had a fantastic profile view as she rubbed suds into breasts and her stomach and down her arms. It was far from a sensual display, but he was so hot for her, she might as well have been giving him a lap dance.

She finished her arms then her hands moved back to her breasts. She cupped them in her hands, her eyes drifting shut as she swirled her thumbs over her nipples. They hardened into two rosy pink points, and he could swear he saw her shudder.

Goddamn.

God knew he'd seen Mel touch herself before. So many times that, honestly, the novelty had sort of worn off. But this was different. Maybe because she didn't know he was watching. Because she wasn't putting on a show for him. She was doing it because it felt good.

She did seem to be enjoying it, and he was so hard his slacks were barely containing him. He watched, loosening his tie as she caressed herself. He tossed it across the back of the toilet and started unbuttoning his shirt.

Melody's hands slipped down off her breasts, then moved slowly south, stroking her hips and her stomach and the tops of her thighs. It was obvious what her final destination would be and he thought, *oh, hell, yeah.* Unfortunately she chose that moment to open her eyes and see him standing there.

She shrieked so loud he was sure the people living beneath them heard it.

"You scared me half to death!" she admonished when she realized it was just him. He half expected her to try to cover herself, but she didn't. Her cheeks did flush though. "How long have you been standing there?"

"Long enough to enjoy what I was seeing."

He could see that she was embarrassed, which made it that much more arousing.

"You know it's rude to spy on people," she said, then her hands came up to cover her breasts. "Tell me you don't have a video camera out there."

He chuckled. "No camera," he assured her, unfastening the buttons at his wrists. "And I wasn't spying, I was watching."

"Same thing."

"You make it sound like I was looking through a peephole in the wall." He tugged the shirt off and dropped it on the floor.

Mel watched it fall, and when she saw the tent in his pants her eyes grew larger. "W-what are you doing?"

He pulled his undershirt over his head and dropped that on the floor, too. "Taking off my clothes."

Her eyes strayed to his chest. He didn't think she realized it, but she was licking her lips. "Um...why?"

"So I can take a shower." He tugged off his socks then unfastened his pants and shoved them and his boxers down.

"With me?" she said, her voice suddenly squeaky and high-pitched, as if she'd been sucking helium.

"Unless you have someone else in there with you."

He crossed the room and pulled the shower door open, his hard-on preceding him inside. If Mel's eyes opened any wider they would fall out of her head.

"I thought we were taking this slow," she said, backing against the far wall, looking worried.

"Don't worry, we are." He stepped under the spray, slicking his hair back. "We're just doing it naked."

If they didn't make love that was okay with him; he just needed to touch her, get his hands on *some* part of her body. If she let him get her off, fantastic, if she returned the favor, even better. He was going to let her set the pace.

Mel stood in the corner watching him, chewing her lip. "This is going to sound stupid, because we've done this before, but I'm really nervous."

"That's why we're taking it slow." And if the anticipation killed him, well, he would at least die with a smile on his face. "So, tell me what you're ready for. What can I do?"

She thought about it for several seconds, then swallowed hard and said, "I guess you could...kiss me."

The logical place to start. He didn't want to corner her, so he took her hand and pulled her to him, so they were both under the spray. But when he leaned in to kiss her, the head of his erection bumped against her stomach. She jumped with surprise, then laughed nervously.

"Outdoor plumbing," he said with a shrug.

"I know, I'm being ridiculous. I'm sorry."

The weird thing was, he liked it. He liked that she wasn't trying to take charge, that for once he could be the aggressor.

"You know what, I have a better idea. Turn around." He grabbed the soap and poured some in his hand.

"What are you going to do?"

"Wash your back." She cast him a wary look, and he said, "Just your back. I promise."

She turned and faced the wall, bracing her hands on the tile as he smoothed the soap across her shoulders and down her back.

"Hmm, that feels nice," she said, as he used both hands to massage her shoulders, and he felt her begin to relax. He worked his way down, but as he got closer to her behind, she tensed again.

"Relax," he said, sliding his hands back up. "This is supposed to be fun."

"I'm sorry. I don't know why I'm so nervous. I wasn't like this in the hotel."

"Maybe it's because you knew you weren't able to do anything then."

She shrugged, and said without much conviction, "Maybe."

His hands stilled. "Why do I get the feeling there's something you're not telling me?"

"It's stupid."

He turned her to face him and she looked so cute, water dripping from her hair, her brow crinkled with the weight of whatever it was that troubled her. "If something is bothering you it's not stupid. If you don't tell me what's really wrong, we can't fix it." And he would *never* get laid.

"It's those videos."

"The shower one?"

She shook her head, eyes on her feet. "The other two. I know it was me, but it's *not* me anymore. That woman... she was just so confident and sexy. I don't think I can do and say the things she did. I can't be her anymore."

He shrugged. "So what?"

Her eyes met his, so full of grief and conflict that he felt his scotch buzz wither away. "I'm *so* afraid I'm going to disappoint you, Ash."

This wasn't one of the silly sex games she used to play with him, or even a mild case of the pre-sex jitters. She was genuinely distraught. He'd never seen her this confused and vulnerable before. Not even in the hospital.

"Mel, you *won't* disappoint me. That's not even a possibility."

She didn't look as though she believed him. She lowered her eyes but he caught her chin in his palm and forced her to look at him. "Listen to me. I don't want the Melody who was in those videos. I want *you*."

He realized it was probably the most honest thing he had ever said to her. He wanted her in a way that he'd never wanted the other Melody.

So why was he still expecting her to act like her? Did he think that, despite being nervous and wanting to go slow, she would just magically shed her inhibitions the instant he touched her?

He wanted her, God knew he did, but not if it was going to hurt or confuse her. It just wasn't worth it. Physically she may have been ready for him, but emotionally she just wasn't there yet. He was pushing too far too fast.

Jesus, when had he gone so soft?

He turned and shut off the water.

"What are you doing?" she asked, looking even more confused, not that he could blame her. First he said they should wait, then he all but molested her, then he put on the brakes again. At this rate he was going to give them both whiplash.

Just because he bought her a car, and planned to give her a couple of credit cards, was he back to thinking she owed him? She hadn't asked for anything.

"We're getting out," he told her.

"But—"

"You're not ready for this. And I'm really sorry that I pushed you. I feel like a total jerk." He didn't just feel like a jerk, he *was* one. He grabbed the towel she'd hung on the hook outside the shower and wrapped it around her, then he got out and fetched one for himself from the linen closet. He fastened it around his hips, and when he turned Melody was standing in the shower doorway, wrapped in her towel, watching him, her brow wrinkled.

"Everything okay?" he asked.

She nodded, but she didn't move.

"We should get dressed. And if the offer for dinner is still good I'd love it if you cooked for me. Or if you prefer we could go out. Your choice."

"Okay," she said, but didn't specify which one, dinner in or out. But before he could ask, she walked out of the bathroom.

He gathered his clothes from the floor and walked into her bedroom, expecting her to be getting dressed. Instead she was lying in bed, propped up on one elbow, the blankets draped about waist level.

She probably wasn't trying to look sexy, but damn it all, she did. At that moment he would swear on his life that she had the most beautiful breasts in the free world. And, God, did he ache to get his hands on them.

"Taking a nap?" he asked.

She shook her head, then she pulled back the covers on the opposite side of the bed and patted the mattress. "Get in."

Get in? Into bed?

Now he was the one who was confused. "Mel—"

"Get in," she said more firmly.

"But…I thought…I thought we were waiting."

"Me, too. Now come over here and get into bed."

Though he still wasn't sure what was going on, he walked to the bed, tossing his clothes in a pile on the floor. His skin was still damp and the sheets stuck to him as he slid between them.

Since he didn't know what she expected from him, he

lay beside her, mirroring her position. "Okay, I'm in. Now what?"

"Now you should kiss me. And this time don't worry about the plumbing. I want you to touch me."

Good, because he started getting hard the second he saw her lying there, and short of putting on pants, or lying on top of the covers while she stayed under them, there was going to be inevitable physical contact. The question was, how far was she willing to let this go?

"Just to be clear, so I don't cross any boundaries, are you saying that you want to make love?"

"Yes, I am. And I do. Right now."

Thank You, God.

She lay back against the pillows, gazing up at him, waiting for his kiss. He knew what the old Mel would expect. She would want it hard and fast and breathless. But this Mel didn't have a clue what she wanted, so he was free to do whatever he chose, like a painter with a clean canvas.

But maybe this time, it was a picture they could paint together.

Twelve

Ash leaned in to kiss her, his hand cupping her face so tenderly, and Melody knew she was safe with him. That she would always be safe.

She wasn't exactly sure what happened in the bathroom, but when Ash shut off the water and wrapped her in a towel, told her they were stopping, something inside her shifted. She knew in that second that she wanted him, that she was ready *now*. It was time to stop looking backward and focus on the future.

His lips brushed hers, so gentle and sweet, and whatever anxiety or fear remained dissolved with their mingling breath. It was the kind of perfect kiss that every girl dreamed about. And she had, she realized. She had been that girl. The memory was so near she could almost reach out and touch it. But she didn't want to think about anything right now, she just wanted to feel. And Ash was exceptional in that department.

His kisses roused her senses and his caresses trailed fire across her skin. It was as if he owned a road map to every erogenous zone on her body, and he explored each one until she felt crazy with want. He made her shudder and quake, taking her to the brink of mindless ecstasy then yanking her back the second before she could reach her peak.

He aroused her with such practiced skill it made her feel inept in her own efforts, but he never once gave the impression that her touch did anything but arouse him. And nothing could be more erotic for her than touching him all over. Learning him again. She discovered that his ears were exceptionally sensitive, because when she nibbled them he groaned and fisted his hands in her hair. And when she did the same to his nipple he dragged her face to his and kissed her so hard she felt breathless. What he seemed to like most though was when she straddled his thighs, took his erection in her hand, but instead of stroking, swirled her thumb in slow circles around the head.

"My God, that feels amazing," Ash said, his eyes rolling closed, his fingers curling into the sheets. It was unbelievably arousing, watching him struggle for control. Knowing she was making him feel that way.

"Did I used to do this to you before?"

He swallowed hard and shook his head. "I don't want to come yet, but if you keep that up I will."

"It's okay if you do." She wanted him to.

He shook his head and opened his eyes. They were glassy and unfocused. "Not yet. Not until I'm inside you."

Well, all he had to do was ask. She rose up on her knees and centered herself over him. When he realized what she intended to do, he asked, "Are you sure?"

She had never been so sure of anything in her life.

Her eyes locked on his, she slowly lowered herself onto his erection, taking him inside her inch by excruciating inch. She was sure that making love, no matter how often or how many times they had done it before, had never given her this soul-deep sensation of completeness.

"You're so *tight*," he said, his hands splayed across her hips, looking as though he was barely hanging on.

She rose up until only the head was inside her, then sank back down. Ash groaned as her body clenched down around him. He reached up and hooked his hands around her neck, pulling her down for a kiss. It was deep and reckless and more than a little wild. And in one smooth motion, he rolled her over so that she was the one on her back, looking up at him. And he was wearing a cocky grin.

She opened her mouth to protest the sudden change of dynamics, but at the same time he rocked into her, swift and deep—*oh, so deep*—and the sound that emerged was a throaty moan.

He pulled back again then rocked forward. Once, twice. Slooowly. Watching her face. This was just like the shower video, only better because she was actually feeling it. And it was everything she expected and more.

Faster, she wanted to say. *Harder.* But the words were getting lost somewhere between her brain and her lips. She felt paralyzed, poised on a precipice, and as he moved inside her, each thrust pushed her a little closer to the edge. Ash must have been able to tell that she was close. He picked up speed.

Her body began to tremble, then quake, then the pleasure took hold almost violently. It felt as though her body was turning in on itself. Toes curling, fingers clenching. She was still in its grip when Ash groaned and shuddered.

She was just starting to come around, to come back to herself, when he dropped his head on her shoulder. He was breathing hard, and she was having a tough time catching her breath, too.

Ash kissed her one last time then rolled over onto the mattress, drawing her against his side.

"Don't take this the wrong way," he said. "But that was without question the quietest sex we have ever had."

She knew from the videos that she had the tendency to be...*vocal,* during sex, but she just assumed she was saucing it up for the camera. She didn't realize she *always* acted that way. "I can try to be louder next time."

"Oh, no," he said quickly. "Quiet is good. I've stopped getting those I-know-what-*you*-did-last-night looks in the elevator."

She rose up on her elbow to look at him. "You're not serious," she said, but she could see by his expression that he was. Her cheeks flushed just thinking about it. He once said that she had voyeuristic tendencies, but come on. "I still have a hard time believing some of the things I did. And you know, I just assumed that when I got my memories back, I would go back to being the person I was before. But the truth is, I don't think I want to. I think I like myself better the way I am now."

"You know, I think I do, too."

She hoped he really meant that. That he wasn't secretly disappointed. "You don't miss the makeup and the perfect hair and the clingy clothes?"

"To be honest, I hadn't given it much thought. The clothes you wear look fine to me, and your hair is cute this way." He reached up and tucked a strand behind her ear. "As for the makeup, I never thought you needed it anyway."

"I think I was insecure as a child."

His brow furrowed. "You remember?"

"Not exactly. It's hard to explain. It's just a feeling I have. I look at the way I was and it's just so not me, so not who I am now. It makes me feel as though I was playing a role. Trying to be something that I wasn't. Which means I couldn't have liked myself very much, could I?"

"I guess not."

"Would it be okay with you if I bought some new clothes? Those lace push-up bras are like medieval torture devices. I'd honestly rather have smaller-looking boobs than suffer another day in one of those things."

He grinned. "You can buy whatever you need."

"I'll probably need you to take me, though. Since I'm not thrilled with the idea of taking the bus. In fact, I may never get on one again. You could just drop me off, and I could call when I'm finished."

"How would you feel about driving yourself?"

She thought about that and realized there was really no reason why she couldn't drive herself. She was off the pain meds and she wasn't getting dizzy any longer. "I guess I could. As long as you don't mind loaning me your car."

He got this adorable, mischievous grin. "I was going to wait until Monday when it got here to tell you."

"When what got here?"

"I wanted it to be a surprise, but I suppose I could tell you now."

"Tell me what?"

He jumped up, looking a bit like an excited little boy, and reached for his pants on the floor. He pulled his cell phone from the pocket, then flopped down on his stomach beside her. He tapped at the touch screen, but when she sat up and tried to see over his shoulder what he was doing, he rolled onto his back. "Just hold on."

He had such a sweet, goofy grin on his face, she was

dying to see what he was up to. When he finally handed her the phone there was photo of a car on the screen. A luxury mini-SUV in a rich shade of blue. "I thought your car was new," she said.

"It is."

"So why buy another one?"

He laughed. "For you. That's your car. Well, not that exact one, but one just like it."

"You bought me a car?"

"You need one, right?"

"Oh, my God." She threw her arms around his neck and hugged him. "Thank you!"

He laughed and hugged her back. "It's not that big of a deal."

"Maybe not to you, but it is to me."

"If you scroll left you can see what it looks at from other angles."

She sat back against the pillows, scrolling through the other shots he'd taken.

"It's so cute! I love it."

"It also has an excellent safety record. And I got the extended option package. It has everything."

She scrolled to the next page, but it wasn't of the car. It took her a second to figure out exactly what it was she was seeing, and when she did, her head began to spin.

One second Mel was all smiles, then her face went slack and all the color leeched from her skin. She lifted a hand to her mouth, as if she might be sick.

He sat up. "Mel, what's wrong?"

She shook her head and said, "I should be dead."

He looked down at his phone and realized she was no longer looking at her new car. She was looking at the photos he'd taken at the impound lot in Texas, of what was left of her old car. He had completely forgotten they were there.

"Crap!" He snatched the phone away, but it was obviously too late. He should have erased the damned things, or at least transferred them to his work computer. "I didn't mean for you to see those. I'm sorry."

She looked up at him, eyes as wide as saucers. "How did I survive that?"

"You were really lucky."

"Everyone kept saying that. But they always say that when someone has an accident and doesn't die. Right?"

He shrugged. "I guess sometimes they really mean it."

"Was it just the one picture, or are there more?"

"Half a dozen maybe. I'll erase them."

She held out her hand. "I want to see."

"Mel—"

"Ash, I *need* to see them."

"It'll just upset you."

"It will upset me more if I don't. *Please.*"

He reluctantly handed it back to her, and watched as she scrolled through the photos. When she got to the last one she scrolled back the other way. She did that a few times, then she closed her eyes tight, as though she was trying to block the image from her mind.

Letting her look had been a bad idea. He should have told her no and erased them. "Mel, why don't you give me—"

"I rolled," she said, eyes still closed.

"That's right. Into a ditch. Then you hit a tree. The doctor told you that, remember?"

Her brow wrinkled in concentration. "The interior was black, the instrument panel had red. Red lights. And the gearshift..." She reached out with her right hand, as if she was touching it. "It was red, too." She opened her eyes and looked up at him. "There was an air freshener hanging from the mirror. It smelled like coconuts."

There was no way she could have seen that kind of detail in the photo on his phone. She was remembering. "What else?"

"I remember rolling." She looked up at him. "I remember being scared, and hurting, and thinking I was going to die. It was…*awful*. But I do remember."

He wondered how long it would take before she remembered what else had happened, *why* she rolled into the ditch. Had she been conscious enough to know that she was miscarrying?

He put his hand on her shoulder. "It's over, and you're safe now."

She looked up at him. "There's something else."

He held his breath.

She stared at him for what felt like an eternity, then she shook her head. "I don't know. I know there's something there. Something I should know. It just won't come."

"It will," he assured her, hoping it never did, wishing she could just be content to let it stay buried.

Thirteen

Mel had a bad dream that night.

After a dinner of takeout Chinese that they both picked at, and a movie neither seemed to be paying much attention to, Ash walked Mel to bed.

He was going to tuck her in then go to his office and work for a while, but she took his hand and said, "Please stay." He couldn't tell her no. They undressed and climbed into bed together. He kissed her goodnight, intending it to be a quick brush of the lips, because he was sure that sex was the last thing on her mind. But her arms went around his neck and she pulled him to her, whispering, "Make love to me again."

He kept waiting for her demanding aggressive side to break through, but she seemed perfectly content lying there, kissing and touching, letting him take the lead. And he realized just how much he preferred this to the hot and heavy stuff.

Afterward she cuddled up against him, warm and soft and limp, and they fell asleep that way. It was a few hours later when she shot up in bed, breath coming in ragged bursts, eyes wild with fear.

He sat up beside her, touched her shoulder, and found that she was drenched in sweat. He felt the sheet and it was drenched, too. For a second he was afraid she'd developed a fever, but her skin was cool.

"I was rolling," she said, her voice rusty from sleep. "I was rolling and rolling and I couldn't stop."

"It was a dream. You're okay." He had no doubt this was a direct result of her seeing those photos and he blamed himself.

"It hurts," she said, cradling her head in her hands. "My head hurts."

He wasn't sure if it hurt now, or she was having a flashback to the accident. She seemed trapped somewhere between dream and sleep. "Do you want a pain pill?"

She shivered and wrapped her arms around herself. "I'm cold."

Well, lying between wet sheets wasn't going to warm her.

"Come on," he said, climbing out of bed and coaxing her to follow him.

"Where?" she asked in a sleepy voice, dutifully letting him lead her into the hall.

"My room. Where it's dry."

He got her tucked in, then laid there for a long time, listening to her slow even breaths, until he finally drifted off.

She apparently didn't remember the dream, or waking up, because she shook him awake the next morning and asked, "Ash, why are we in your bedroom?"

"You had a nightmare," he mumbled, too sleepy to even open his eyes.

"I did?"

"The sheets were sweaty so I moved us in here." He thought she may have said something else after that but he had already drifted back to sleep. When he woke again it was after eight, far later than he usually got up. Even on a Sunday. He would have to skip the gym and go straight to work.

He showered and dressed in slacks and a polo since it was Sunday and it was doubtful anyone else would be around the office, then went out to the kitchen. Mel was sitting on the couch wearing jeans and a T-shirt, her hair pulled back in a ponytail, knees pulled up with her feet propped on the cushion in front of her. If he didn't know better, he would say she wasn't a day over eighteen.

When she saw him she looked up and smiled. "Good morning."

He walked to the back of the couch and leaned over, intending to kiss her cheek, but she turned her head and caught his lips instead. They tasted like coffee, and a hint of something sweet—a pastry maybe—and she smelled like the soap they had used in the shower last night. He was damned tempted to lift her up off the couch, toss her over his shoulder and take her back to bed.

Maybe later.

When he broke the kiss she was still smiling up at him.

"Good morning," he said.

"There's coffee."

"How long have you been up?" he asked as he walked to the kitchen. She'd already set a cup out for him.

"Six-thirty." She followed him into the kitchen, taking

a seat on one of the bar stools at the island. "It was a little disorienting waking up in a bed I didn't fall asleep in."

"You still don't remember it?"

She shook her head. "I do remember something else though. The book I've been reading, I've read it before. I mean, I figured I had, since it was on the shelf. But I picked it up this morning after already reading almost half of it, and bam, suddenly I remember how it ended. So I went to the bookshelf and looked at a few others, and after I read the back blurb, and skimmed the first few pages, I remembered those, too."

This was bound to happen. He just hadn't expected it to be this soon. "Sounds like you've been busy."

"Yeah. I was sitting there reading those books, thinking how stupid it was that I could remember something so immaterial, and I couldn't even remember my own mother. Then it hit me. The picture."

"What picture?"

"The one of me and my mom, when I was thirteen."

He recalled seeing it in her room before, but not since they had been back. He didn't recall seeing it in her place in Texas either. "I remember you having one, but I don't know where it is."

"That's okay. I remembered. It just popped into my head. I knew it was in the front pouch of my suitcase. And it was."

Ash could swear his heart stopped, then picked up triple time. She remembered packing? "Your suitcase?"

"I figured I must have taken it with me on my trip."

"Right…you must have." Hadn't he checked her suit-cases? So there would be nothing to jolt her memory? It was possible that he only patted the front pouches, assuming they were empty.

Oh, well, it was just a photo.

"I found something else, too," she said, and there was something about her expression, the way she was looking at him, that made his heart slither down to his stomach. She pulled a folded-up piece of paper from her back pocket and handed it to him.

He unfolded it and realized immediately what it was. A lease, for her rental in Abilene.

Oh, hell. He should have checked the damned outer pockets.

"I wasn't on a research trip, was I?"

He shook his head.

"I moved out, didn't I? I left you."

He nodded.

"I've been sitting here, trying to remember what happened, why I left, but it's just not there."

Which meant she didn't remember the affair, or the child. The limb-weakening relief made him feel like a total slime. But as long as she didn't remember, he could just pretend it never happened. Or who knew, maybe she did remember, and she was content to keep it her little secret. As long as they didn't acknowledge it, it didn't exist.

"You didn't leave a note," he said. "I just came home from work one day and you were gone. I guess you weren't happy."

She frowned. "I just took off and you didn't come after me?"

"Not at first," he admitted, because at this point lying to her would only make things worse. "I was too angry. And too proud, I guess. I convinced myself that after a week or two you would change your mind and come back. I thought you would be miserable without me. But you didn't come back, and I was the one who was miserable. So I hired the P.I."

"And you found out that I was in the hospital?"

He nodded. "I flew to Texas the next morning. I was going to talk you into coming back with me."

"But I had amnesia. So you told me I had been on a trip."

He nodded. "I was afraid that if I told you the truth, you wouldn't come home. I went to your rental and packed your things and had them shipped back here. And I..." Jeez, this was tough. They were supposed to be having this conversation when he was dumping her, and reveling in his triumph. He wasn't supposed to fall for her.

"You what?" she asked.

"I..." *Christ, just say it, Ash.* "I went through your computer. I erased a lot of stuff. Things I thought would jog your memory. E-mails, school stuff, music."

She nodded slowly, as though she was still processing it, trying to decide if she should be angry with him. "But you did it because you were afraid of losing me."

"Yes." More or less, anyway. Just not for the reason she thought. And if he was going to come this far, he might as well own up to all of it. "There's one more thing."

She took a deep breath, as if bracing herself. "Okay."

"It's standard procedure that hospitals will only give out medical information to next of kin. Parents, spouses... *fiancés...*"

It took a minute for her to figure it out, and he could tell the instant it clicked. He could see it in her eyes, in the slow shake of her head. "We're not engaged."

"It was the only way I could get any information. The only way the doctor would talk to me."

She had this look on her face, as if she might be sick. He imagined he was wearing a similar expression.

She slid her ring off and set it on the counter. At least she didn't throw it at him. "I guess you'll be wanting this back. Although, I don't imagine it's real."

"No, it's real. It's…" God, this was painful. "It's my ex-wife's."

She took a deep breath, holding in what had to be seething anger. He wished she would just haul off and slug him. They would both feel better. Not that he deserved any absolution of guilt.

"But you did it because you were afraid of losing me," she said, giving him an out.

"Absolutely." And despite feeling like the world's biggest ass, telling her the truth lifted an enormous weight off his shoulders. He felt as though he could take a full breath for the first time since the day he had walked into her hospital room.

"You can't even imagine how guilty I've felt," he told her.

"Is this why you've been avoiding me?"

Her words stunned him. "What do you mean?"

"All the late nights at work."

"I always work late. I always have."

"Do you always tell me you're at work when you really aren't?"

What was she talking about? "I've never done that. If I said I was at work, that's where I was."

"I called your office yesterday afternoon, to ask you about dinner, but you didn't answer. I left a message, too, but you never called back."

He could lie about it, say he was making copies or in a meeting or something, but the last thing he needed was one more thing to come back at him. "I was there. Brock and Flynn decided to throw an impromptu party. To celebrate our engagement."

Her eyes widened a little. "Well, that must have been awkward."

"You have no idea."

"I guess that's my fault, for spilling the beans."

"Mel, none of this is even close to your fault. I find the fact that you haven't thrown something at me a miracle."

"In a way, I feel like I should be thanking you."

"For what?"

"If you hadn't done this, I would never have known how happy I could be with you."

Not in a million years would he expect her to thank him for lying to her.

"But," she continued, and he felt himself cringe. When there was a but, it was never good. "If things stay the way they are, you're going to lose me again."

This was no empty threat. He could see that she was dead serious.

"What things?"

"You're always at work. You're gone before I get up and you come home after I'm asleep. That might be easier to stomach if you at least took the weekends off. I sort of feel like, what's the point of being together, if we're never together?"

The old Melody would have never complained about the dynamics of their relationship, or how many hours he worked. Even if it did bother her. And maybe that was part of the problem.

He couldn't deny that right before she left, he had been pulling away from her. He was almost always at work, either at Maddox, or in his home office. And it seemed that the further he retreated, the harder she tried to please him, until she was all but smothering him. Then, boom, she was gone.

Had it never occurred to him that he had all but driven her into another man's arms?

He knew that the sugar daddy/mistress arrangement wasn't an option any longer. She wanted the real thing.

She deserved it. But what did he want? Was he ready for that kind of commitment?

He thought about Melody and how she used to be, and how she was now. There was no longer a good Melody and an evil one. She was the entire package. She was perfect just the way she was, and he realized that if he ever were to settle down again, he could easily imagine himself with her. But relationships took compromise and sacrifice, and he was used to pretty much always getting his way, never having to work at it.

And honestly, he'd been bored out of his skull.

He wanted a woman who could think for herself, and be herself, even if that meant disappointing him sometimes, or disagreeing with him.

He wanted Melody.

"Mel, after everything I went through to get you back, do you honestly think I would just let you go again?"

Her bottom lip started to tremble and her eyes welled, though she was trying like hell to hold it back. But he didn't want her holding anything back.

He walked around the island to her but she was already up and meeting him halfway. She threw herself around him and he wrapped her up in his arms.

This was a good thing they had. A really good thing. And this time he was determined not to screw it up.

After seeing the pictures of her wrecked car, Melody's memories began to come back with increasing frequency. Random snippets here and there. Things like the red tennis shoes she had gotten on her birthday when she was five, and rides her mother let her take on the pony outside the grocery store.

She remembered her mother's unending parade of boyfriends and husbands. All of them mistreated her mother in some way or another, often physically. She didn't seem to know how to stand up for herself, when to say *enough,* yet when it came to protecting Mel, she was fierce. Mel remembered when one of them came after her. She couldn't have been more than ten or eleven. She remembered standing frozen in place, too frightened to even shield her face as he approached her with an open palm, arm in mid-swing. She closed her eyes, waiting for the impact, then she heard a thud and opened her eyes to find him kneeling on the floor, stunned and bleeding from his head, and her mother hovering over him with a baseball bat.

She hadn't been a great mother, but she had kept Mel safe.

Despite having finally learned that it was socially unacceptable, Mel had been so used to the idea of men hitting that when she'd started seeing Ash she'd always been on guard, waiting for the arm to swing. But after six months or so, when he hadn't so much as raised his voice to her, she'd realized that he would never hurt her. Not physically anyway.

When she admitted that to Ash, instead of being insulted, he looked profoundly sad. They lay in bed after making love and talked about it. About what her life had been like as a child, how most of her memories were shrouded in fear and insecurity. And as she opened up to him, Ash miraculously began to do the same.

She recalled enough to know that their relationship had never been about love, and that for those three years they had been little more than roommates. Roommates who had sex. She couldn't help but feel ashamed that she had compromised herself for so long, that she hadn't insisted on better. But they were in a real relationship now. They had a future. They talked and laughed and spent time together.

They saw movies and had picnics and took walks on the shore. They were a couple.

He didn't care that her hair was usually a mess and her clothes didn't cling. Or that she'd stopped going to the gym and lost all those pretty muscles and curves she'd worked so hard to maintain, and now was almost as scrawny as she'd been in high school. *Less is more,* he had said affectionately when she'd complained that she had no hips and her butt had disappeared. He didn't even miss the push-up bras, although he knew damn well if that had been a prerequisite to the relationship she probably would have walked.

He even forgave her for all the orgasms she had faked, during sex she didn't want but had anyway, because she was so afraid of disappointing him. And she was humbled to learn that there were many nights when he would have been happy to forgo the sex and watch a movie instead. He made her promise that she would never have sex if she didn't want to, and she swore to him that she would never fake an orgasm again. He promised that she would never need to, and in the weeks that passed, she didn't.

Despite all the talking they had done, there was still one thing that they hadn't discussed, something she had been afraid to bring up. Because as close as they had grown, there was still that little girl inside who was afraid to disappoint him. But she knew she had waited long enough, and one morning at breakfast, over eggs and toast, he gave her the perfect segue.

"Since your memory is almost completely back now, have you considered when you'll go back to school?" he asked.

She was suddenly so nervous that the juice she was drinking got caught in her throat. It was now or never.

"Not really," she said, then thought, *Come on, Mel, be*

brave. Just tell him the truth. "The thing is, I don't want to go back. I don't want to be a lawyer."

He shrugged and said, "Okay," then he took a drink of his juice and went back to eating.

She was so stunned her mouth actually fell open. All that worrying, all the agonizing she had done over this, and all he had to say was *okay?*

She set her fork down beside her plate. "Is that it?"

He looked up from the toast he was spreading jam on. "Is what it?"

"I say I don't want to be a lawyer and all you say is *okay?*"

He shrugged. "What do you want me to say?"

"After you spent all that money on law-school tuition, doesn't it upset you that I'm just going to throw my education away?"

"Not really. An education isn't worth much if you aren't happy in what you're doing."

If she had known he would be so understanding she would have told him the truth months and months ago. She thought of all the time she had wasted on a career path that had been going nowhere. If only she'd had the courage to open up to him.

"Do you have any idea what you might want to do?" he asked.

The million-dollar question.

"I think so."

When she didn't elaborate he said, "Would you like to tell me?"

She fidgeted with her toast, eyes on her plate. "I was thinking, maybe I can stay home for a while."

"That's fine. It isn't like you *need* to work."

"Maybe I could do something here, instead of an outside job."

"Like a home business?"

"Sort of." *Just say it, Mel. Spit it out.* "But one that involves things like midnight feedings and diaper changes."

He brow dipped low. He took a deep breath and exhaled slowly. "Mel, you know I can't—"

"I know. I do. But there's always artificial means. Or even adoption. And I don't mean right now. I would want us to be married first." He opened his mouth to say something but she held up a hand to stop him. "I know we haven't discussed anything definite, or made plans, and I'm not trying to rush things. I swear. I just wanted to sort of…put it out there, you know, to make sure we're on the same page."

"I didn't know you wanted kids."

"I didn't either. Not till recently. I always told myself I would never want to put a kid through what I went through. I guess I just assumed I would have a life like my mom's. It never occurred to me that I would ever meet someone like you."

A faint smile pulled at the corners of his mouth, but he hid it behind a serious look. "How many kids are we talking about?"

Her heart leaped up and lodged somewhere in her throat. At least he was willing to discuss it. "One or two. Or *maybe* three."

He raised a brow.

"Or just two."

After a pause he said, "And this is something you *really* want?"

She bit her lip and nodded. "I really do."

There was another long pause, and for a second she was afraid he would say no. Not just afraid. She was terrified.

Because this *could* be a deal breaker. She wanted a family. It was all she'd been able to think about lately.

"Well," he finally said. "I guess one of each would be okay."

By the time the last word left his mouth she was already around the table and in his lap with her arms around his neck. "Thank you!"

He laughed and hugged her. "But not until we're married, and you know I don't want to rush into anything."

"I know." They could hardly call three years rushing, but she knew Ash had trust issues. After his own cancer, then losing his mother to the disease, he'd had a hard time letting himself get close to people, then when he finally did, and married his wife, she had betrayed him in the worst way possible.

But Ash had to know by now that she would never do that to him. She loved him, and she knew that he loved her, even if he hadn't said the words yet.

It was a big step for him, but she knew if she was patient he would come around.

Fourteen

Ash sat at his desk at work, still smiling to himself about the irony of Mel's timing. Funny that she would pick today to finally broach the marriage and kids subject, when tonight he planned to take her out for a romantic dinner, followed by a stroll by the water, where, at sunset, he would drop down on one knee and ask her to marry him.

He hoped that if she had even the slightest suspicion of his intentions, he had dispelled that when he pretended not to be sure about wanting kids. Although admittedly, until recently anyway, he hadn't even considered it. He'd never planned to get tied down again, so it had just naturally never entered his mind. And his ex had never expressed a desire for children.

Now he knew, if they were his and Mel's, his life would never be complete without them. Natural or adopted.

He opened his top drawer, pulled out the ring box and flipped the top up. It wasn't as flashy as the ring he'd given his ex. The stone was smaller and the setting more traditional, but after Mel confessed how much she had disliked the ring for their fake engagement, he knew she would love this one. A sturdy ring, the jeweler had told him, one that would hold up through diaper changes and baby baths and dirty laundry. And with any luck that would be the scene at their condo for the next several years.

There was a knock on his office door. Ash closed the ring box and set it back in his drawer just as Gavin Spencer stuck his head in. "Am I bothering you?"

"Nothing that can't wait," Ash said, gesturing him in.

Gavin strode over and sank into the chair opposite Ash's desk. "It's getting really weird out there."

Ash didn't have to ask what he meant. The mood around the office had been tense for the past couple of weeks. He could only assume it was due in part to the security leaks. It wasn't openly discussed, but at this point everyone knew.

"That's why I stay in here," Ash said.

"You're lucky you can. You should try working with Logan Emerson."

"I did notice that he doesn't exactly seem to fit in."

"He kind of creeps me out," Gavin said. "It seems like every time I look up, he's watching me. Then I caught him in my office the other day. He said he was leaving me a memo."

"Did he?"

"Yeah. But I could swear the papers on my desk had been moved around. There's something not quite right with him. There are times when he doesn't even seem to know what the hell he's doing. Doesn't seem like a very smart hire to me. If it were my firm, you could bet I would do things differently."

But it wasn't. He knew Gavin dreamed of branching

out on his own, of being the boss, but talk like that could make some people nervous. Ash just hoped Gavin wouldn't undermine the integrity of Maddox and leak information to Golden Gate to suit his own interests.

Gavin's cell rang and when he looked at the display he shot up from his chair. "Damn, gotta take this. I've got a lead on a new client. I don't want to say too much, but it could be very lucrative."

"Well, good luck."

When Gavin was gone Ash looked at the clock. It seemed that time was crawling by today. It was still four hours until he picked up Mel for dinner. It was going to be tough sitting through the entire meal, knowing the ring was in his pocket. But he knew that the water was one of her favorite places, so that was where he wanted to do it. He'd timed it so that the sun would be setting and the view would be spectacular.

He'd planned it so precisely, there wasn't a single thing that could possibly go wrong.

Melody was running late.

She leaned close to the mirror and fixed the eyeliner smudge in the corner of her eye. Boy, she was out of practice.

Ash stuck his head in for tenth time in the past fifteen minutes. "Ready yet?"

"One more minute."

"That's what you said ten minutes ago. We're going to be late for our reservation."

"The restaurant isn't going anywhere. It won't kill us if we have to wait a little longer." It was their first real night out since the accident, and she wanted it to be special. She'd bought a new dress and even curled her hair and pinned it up.

"Mel?"

"Fine! Jeez." She swiped on some lipstick, dropped the tube in her purse and said, "Let's go."

He hustled her into the elevator, then into the car. Her new car sat beside his, and though she had been a little nervous at first being back in the driver's seat, now she loved it. She even made excuses to go out just so she could drive it.

Ash got in the driver's side, started the car and zipped through the garage to the entrance. He made a right out onto the street. Traffic was heavy, and Ash cursed when they had to stop at the red light.

"We're going to be late," he complained, watching for a break in the traffic so he could hang a right.

"What is it with you tonight?" she asked, pulling down the mirror on the visor to check her eyeliner one last time. "Are you going to turn into a pumpkin or something?"

He started to move forward just as she was flipping her visor up, and at the same time a guy on a bike shot off the curb and into the intersection.

"Ash!" she screamed, and he slammed on the brakes, barely missing the guy's back tire as he flew by in an attempt to beat the light.

"Idiot," Ash muttered, then he turned to look at her. "You okay?"

She couldn't answer. Her hands were trembling and braced on the dash, her breath coming in short, fast bursts. She suddenly felt as though her heart was going to explode from her chest it was hammering so hard.

"Mel? Talk to me," Ash said, sounding worried, but his voice was garbled, as if he was talking to her through water.

She tried, but she couldn't talk. Her lips felt numb and she wasn't getting enough air.

Out. She had to get out of the car.

The car behind them honked so Ash zipped around the corner.

He put his hand on her arm, keeping one eye on her and one on the road. "Mel, you're scaring me."

She couldn't breathe. She was trapped and she needed air.

She reached for the door handle and yanked, not even caring that they were still moving, but the door was locked.

Ash saw what she was doing and yanked her away from the door. "Jesus, Mel, what are you doing?"

"Out," she wheezed, still struggling to get a breath. "Get me out."

"Hold on," he said, gripping her arm, genuine fear in his voice. "Let me pull over."

He whipped down the alley behind their building then turned back into the parking garage. The second he came to a stop she clawed her door open and threw herself out, landing on her knees on the pavement. Her purse landed beside her and its contents spilled out, but she didn't care. She just needed air.

She heard Ash's door open and in an instant he was behind her. "Mel, what happened? Is it your head? Are you hurt?"

It was getting easier to breathe now, but that crushing panic, the instinct to run intensified as adrenaline raced through her bloodstream.

She closed her eyes, but instead of blackness she saw a rain-slicked windshield, she heard the steady thwap of the wipers. The weather was getting worse, she thought. Better get home. But then there was a bike. One second it wasn't there, then it was, as though it materialized from thin air. She saw a flash of long blond hair, a pink hoodie. She yanked the wheel, there was a loud thunk, then rolling—

"No!" Her eyes flew open. She was still in the parking garage, on the floor. But it happened. It was real. "I hit her. I hit the girl."

"Mel, you have to calm down," Ash said sternly, then she felt his arms around her, helping her up off the ground. Her knees were so weak, her legs so shaky she could hardly walk on her own.

"There was a bike," she told him. "And a girl. I hit her."

"Let's get you upstairs," he said, helping her to the elevator.

As the doors slid shut she closed her eyes and was suddenly overwhelmed by the sensation that she was rolling. Rolling and rolling, violent thrashing, pain everywhere, then wham. A sharp jolt and a pain in her head. Then, nothing. No movement. No sound.

Can't move.

Trapped.

"Mel."

Her eyes flew open.

"We're here."

Disoriented, she gazed around and realized she was back in the elevator, on their floor and he was nudging her forward. Not in the car. Not trapped.

He helped her inside and sat her down on the couch. He poured her a drink and pressed it into her hands. "Drink this. It'll help you calm down."

She lifted it to her lips and forced herself to take a swallow, nearly gagging as it burned a trail of fire down her throat. But she was feeling better now. Not so panicked. Not so afraid. The fuzziness was gone.

He started to move away and she gripped the sleeve of his jacket. "Don't go!"

"I'm just going to get the first-aid kit from the guest bathroom. We need to clean up your knees."

She looked down and saw that her knees were raw and oozing blood, and the sight of it made her feel dizzy and sick to her stomach.

She lay back and let her head fall against the cushion. She remembered now, as clear as if it had happened this morning. She was in the car, knowing she had to get help. She had to help the girl. But when she tried to move her arms something was pinning her. She was trapped. She tried to see what it was, thinking she could pry it loose, but the second she moved her head, pain seized with a vicelike grip, so intense that bile rose up to choke her. She moaned and closed her eyes against the pain.

She tried to think, tried to concentrate on staying conscious. Then she felt it, low in her belly. A sharp pain. Then cramping. She remembered thinking, *No, not there. Not the baby.*

The baby.

Oh, God. She had been pregnant. She was going to have Ash's baby.

The final piece of the puzzle slid into place. That was why she left Ash. That was why she ran to Texas. She was pregnant with Ash's baby, a baby she knew he would never want.

The relief of finally having the answers, finally seeing the whole picture, paled in comparison to the ache in her heart.

They could have been a family. She and Ash and the baby. They could have been happy. But how could she have known?

Ash reappeared and knelt down in front of her. He'd

taken off his suit jacket and rolled his sleeves to his elbows. "This is probably going to sting," he warned her, then he used a cool, damp washcloth to wipe away the blood. She sucked in a surprised breath as she registered the raw sting of pain.

"Sorry," he said. "This probably won't feel much better, but we don't want it getting infected. God only knows what's on the floor down there."

He wet a second cloth with hydrogen peroxide, and she braced herself against the pain as he dabbed it on her knees. It went white and bubbly on contact.

If she had known it could be like this, that they could be so happy, she wouldn't have left. She would have told him about the baby.

Now it was too late.

Ash smoothed a jumbo-size bandage across each knee. "All done."

"Is she dead?" Mel asked him, as he busied himself with repacking the first-aid kit. The fact that he wouldn't look at her probably wasn't a good sign. "Please tell me."

He sighed deeply and looked up at her. "It wasn't your fault."

So that was a yes. She pretty much knew already. And her fault or not, she had killed someone's baby. Someone's child. And she hadn't even had a chance to apologize. To say she was sorry. "Why didn't someone tell me?"

"The doctor thought it would be too traumatic."

She laughed wryly. "And finding out this way has just been a barrel of laughs."

He rose to his feet, the kit and soiled rags in hand. "He did what he thought was best."

It hit her suddenly that the doctor must have told him about the baby, too. He thought Ash was her fiancé. What reason would he have to hide it?

All this time Ash knew and he had never said a word. It was one thing to lie about engagements, and hide personal information, but this was their *child*.

"Is that why you didn't say anything about the baby, either?"

Ash closed his eyes and shook his head. "Don't do this. Just let it go."

"Let it go? I lost a baby."

He looked at her, his eyes pleading. "Everything has been so good, please don't ruin it."

"Ruin it?"

"Can't we just do what we've been doing and pretend it never happened?"

Her mouth fell open. "How can you even say something like that? I lost a child—"

"That wasn't mine!" he shouted, slamming the first-aid kit down so hard on the coffee table that she heard the glass crack. She was so stunned by the unprecedented outburst that it took a second for his words to sink in.

"Ash, who told you it wasn't yours? Of course it was yours."

He leveled his eyes on her, and if she didn't know better, she would think he was going to hit her. But when he spoke his voice was eerily calm. "You and I both know that's impossible. I'm sterile."

She could hardly believe what he was suggesting. "You think I had an *affair*."

"I had unprotected sex with you for three years, and with my wife for seven years, and no one got pregnant before now, so yeah, I think it's pretty damn likely that you had an affair."

He couldn't honestly believe she would do that. "Ash, since that night at the party, when we met, there has been *no one* but you."

"The party? I seriously doubt that."

He might as well have just called her a whore.

"If it *was* mine," he said, "why did you run off?"

"Because you had made it pretty clear that you had no desire to have a family, and you sure as hell didn't seem to want me. I figured it would be best for everyone if I just left. Frankly, I'm surprised you even noticed I was gone."

His eyes cut sharply her way.

Why was he being so stubborn? He *knew* her. He knew she would never hurt him. "Ash, I'm telling you the *truth*."

"And I'm just supposed to trust you? Just take your word for it when I know it's impossible?"

"Yes. You should. Because you know I wouldn't lie to you."

"I don't believe you," he said, and it felt as though a chunk of her heart broke away.

"Why did you even bring me back here? If you thought I cheated on you, if you hated me that much, why not just leave me in the hospital? Were you plotting revenge or something?"

His jaw clenched and he looked away.

She was just being surly, but she'd hit the nail right on the head. "Oh, my God." She rose from the couch. "You *were*, weren't you? You wanted to get back at me."

He turned to her, eyes black with anger. "After all I did for you, you betrayed me. I've taken care of you for three years, and you repay me by screwing around. You're damn right I wanted revenge." He shook his head in disgust. "You want to know the really pathetic thing? I forgave you. I thought you had changed. I was going to ask you to marry me tonight, for real this time. But here you are, *still* lying to me. Why won't you just admit what you did? Own up to it."

Own up to something she didn't do?

The really sad thing was that she suspected, somewhere deep down, he believed her. He knew she was telling the truth. He just didn't want to hear it. When the chips were down, and things got a little tough, it was easier to push her away than take a chance.

"Is this the way it is with you?" she asked. "You find something really good, but when you get too close, you throw it away? Is that what you did to your wife? Did you ignore her for so long that you drove her away?"

He didn't respond, but she could see that she'd hit a nerve.

"I love you, Ash. I wanted to spend the rest of my life with you, but I just can't fight for you anymore."

"No one asked you to."

And that pretty much said it all. "Give me an hour to pack my things. And I would appreciate if I could use the car for a couple of weeks, until I can find another one."

"Keep it," he said.

Like a parting gift? she wondered. Or the booby prize.

She rose from the couch and walked to her room to pack, her legs still wobbly from the adrenaline rush, her knees sore.

But they didn't even come close to the pain in her heart.

Ash sat at a booth in the Rosa Lounge, sipping his scotch, trying to convince himself that he wasn't miserable, wasn't a complete idiot, and not doing a very good job of it.

Mel had been gone three days and he could barely stand

it. And now that he finally realized what an idiot he'd been, he wasn't sure how to fix it.

He knew he had to be pretty desperate at this point to arrange this meeting, but there were some things that Mel had said that really stuck in his craw, and he had to know, once and for all, if she was right.

He checked his watch again and looked over at the door just in time to see her come in. Her hair was shorter than before, but otherwise she didn't look all that different. She scanned the room and he rose from his seat, waving her over. When she saw him, she smiled, which was a good sign. When he'd called her and asked to meet she'd sounded a little wary.

As she walked to the booth he saw that she still looked really good, and, wow, really pregnant.

"Linda," he said as she approached. "Good to see you."

"Hello, Ash." His ex-wife leaned in and air kissed his cheek. "You look great."

"You, too," he said. "Please sit down."

He waited until she slid into the opposite side of the booth, then he sat, too.

The waitress appeared to take her drink order, and when she was gone Ash gestured to Linda's swollen middle. "You're pregnant. I had no idea."

She placed a hand on her stomach and smiled. "Six weeks to go."

"Congratulations. You're still with…" He struggled to conjure up a name.

"Craig," she supplied for him. "We just celebrated our second wedding anniversary last month."

"That's great. You look very happy."

"I am," she said with a smile. "Everything is going great. I don't know if you remember, but Craig owned a gym in our old neighborhood. I talked him into expanding and we just opened our fourteenth fitness center."

"I'm glad to hear it."

"How about you? What have you been up to?"

"I'm still at Maddox."

She waited, as if she expected more, and when there wasn't she asked, "Anyone...*special* in your life?"

"For a while," he said, wanting to add, *until I royally screwed up.* "It's complicated."

She waited for him to elaborate. And though he hadn't planned to, the words just kind of came out.

"We just split up," he heard himself tell her. "A few days ago, in fact."

"I'm going to go out on a limb and assume that you asking to meet me is directly related somehow."

His cx was no dummy.

"I need to ask you something," he told her, rubbing his hands together, wondering if maybe this wasn't such a good idea. "And it's probably going to sound...well, a little weird after all this time."

"Okay." She folded her hands in front of her and leaned forward slightly, giving him her undivided attention.

"I need to know why you did it. Why you cheated on me."

He thought she might be offended or defensive, but she looked more surprised than upset. "Wow, okay. I didn't see that one coming."

"I'm not trying to play the blame game, I swear. I just really need to know."

"You're sure you want to do this?"

No, but he'd come this far and there was no going back now. "I'm sure. I need to know."

"Let's face it, Ash, by the time you caught me with Craig, our marriage had been over for a long time. It was only a matter of time before I left. You just didn't want to see it, didn't want to take responsibility. You wanted to make me out to be the monster."

"I guess I still believed we were happy."

"Happy? We were nonexistent. You were never around, and even when you were you were a ghost. You just didn't want to see it."

She was right. They had drifted apart. He didn't want to see it. Didn't want to take the blame.

"I know it was wrong to cheat on you, and I'll always be truly sorry for that. I didn't want to hurt you, but I was so lonely, Ash. The truth is, when you caught us, and you were so angry, I was stunned. I honestly didn't think you cared anymore. I felt as though I could have packed my bags and left, and you wouldn't have noticed until you ran out of clean underwear."

All of this was beginning to sound eerily familiar.

"So I drove you to it?"

"Please don't think that I'm placing all the blame on you. I could have tried harder, too. I could have insisted you take more time for me. I just assumed we were in a phase, that we had drifted, and eventually we would meet back up somewhere in the middle again. I guess by the time it got really bad, it didn't seem worth saving. I just didn't love you anymore."

"Wow," he said. Drive the knife in deeper.

"Ash, come on, you can't honestly say you didn't feel the same way."

She was right. His pride had taken a much bigger hit than his heart.

"Is that what you wanted to know?" she asked.

He smiled. "Yeah. I appreciate your honesty."

She cringed suddenly and pushed down on the top of

her belly. "Little bugger is up under my ribs again. I think he's going to be a soccer player."

"He?"

"Yeah. We still haven't settled on a name. I'm partial to Thomas, and Craig likes Jack."

"I always thought you didn't want kids."

"It's not so much that I didn't want them, but it never seemed like the right time. And it was a touchy subject for you, since you thought you couldn't."

"*Thought* I couldn't?"

She frowned, as though she realized she'd said something she shouldn't have.

"Linda?"

She looked down at her hands. "I probably should have told you before."

Why did Ash get the feeling he wasn't going to like this? "Told me what?"

"It was in college. We had been together maybe six months. I found out I was pregnant. And before you ask, yes, it was yours."

"But I can't—"

"Believe me, you can. And you did. But we were both going for degrees, and we hadn't even started talking about marriage at that point. Not to mention that we had student loans up the yin yang. I knew it was *really* lousy timing. So I did what I believed was the best thing for both of us and had an abortion."

Ash's head was spinning so violently he nearly fell out of the booth. "But all those years we didn't use protection?"

"*You* didn't, but I did. I had an IUD. So there wouldn't be any more accidents."

He could hardly believe he was hearing this. "Why didn't you tell me?"

"I thought I was protecting you. Believe me when I say I felt guilty enough for the both of us. And even if I had wanted to keep the baby, I knew you wouldn't. I didn't want to burden you with that."

That seemed to be a common theme when it came to him and women.

So Mel had been telling him the truth. She had been through hell and lived to talk about it, she had lost a baby, *his* baby, and he had more or less accused her of being a tramp.

He could have been a father. And he would have, if he hadn't been so selfish and blind. Not to mention *stupid*.

He closed his eyes and shook his head. "I am such an idiot."

"Why do I get the feeling you're not talking about us any longer?"

He looked over at her. "Do you think some people are destined to keep repeating their mistakes?"

"Some people maybe. If they don't learn from them."

"And if they learn too late?"

She reached across the table and laid her hand over his, and just like that, all the unresolved conflict, all the bitterness he'd shouldered for the past three years seemed to vanish. "Do you love her?" she asked.

"Probably too much for my own good."

"Does she love you?"

"She did three days ago."

She grinned and gave his hand a squeeze. "So what the heck are you doing still sitting here with me?"

Damn, the woman was good at disappearing. He had no clue where she was staying and she refused to answer her phone. But this time Ash didn't wait nearly as long to call the P.I. and ask him to find her again. But when Ash gave him the make and year of her car, the P.I. asked, "Does the car have GPS?"

"Yeah, it does."

"Then you don't really need me. You can track her every move on any computer. Or even your phone if it has Internet. I can help you set it up."

"That would be great," Ash told him. It was about time something went right. And thank God this time she hadn't gone very far. Within hours he was pulling into the lot of a grocery store a few miles away from the condo.

The idea of a confrontation inside the store seemed like a bad idea, so he parked, got out of his car and made himself comfortable on her hood. There was no way she would be leaving without at least talking to him.

She came out of the store maybe ten minutes later and his heart lifted at the sight of her, then it lodged in his throat when he thought of all the explaining he had to do. And the confessing.

She had one bag in her arms and she was rooting around in her purse for something, so she didn't see him right away.

She looked adorable with her hair up in a ponytail, wearing jeans, tennis shoes and a pullover sweatshirt. He was finding it hard to imagine what he considered so appealing in the way she looked before the accident. This just seemed to be a better fit.

She was almost to the car when she finally looked up and noticed him there. Her steps slowed and her eyes narrowed. He could see that she was wondering how he'd found her, especially when she had been dodging his calls.

"GPS," he said. "I tracked you on my phone."

"You realize that stalking is a criminal offense in California?"

"I don't think it can be considered stalking when I technically own the car."

She tossed the keys at him so forcefully that if he hadn't caught them he might have lost an eye. "Take it," she said and walked past him in the direction of the street.

He jumped down off the hood to follow her. "Come on, Mel. I just want to talk to you."

"But I don't want to listen. I'm still too mad at you."

Mad was good as far as he was concerned. Since he deserved it. She could get over being mad at him a lot easier than, say, hating his guts. Not that he didn't deserve that, too.

She was walking so fast he had to jog to catch up to her. "I've been an ass."

She snorted. "You say that like it's something I don't already know."

"But do you know how sorry I am?"

"I'm sure you are."

"It's not that I didn't believe you about the baby. I just didn't want it to be true."

She stopped so abruptly he nearly tripped over his own feet. "Are you actually saying that you didn't want it to be yours?"

"No! Of course not."

"You really are an ass," she said, and turned to leave, but he grabbed her arm.

"Would you please listen for a minute? I could live with the idea that you'd had an affair, that you had made a mistake, especially when I was the one who drove you away in the first place. But knowing that the baby was mine, and I was responsible…" Emotion welled up in his throat and he had to pause to get a hold of himself. "If I had treated you right, showed you that I loved you, you never would have felt like you had to run away. All the terrible things you went through never would have happened. Everything, all of it, is *my* fault."

She was quiet for what seemed like a very long time, and he watched her intently, in case she decided to throw something else at him. God only knew what she had in the bag.

"It's no one's," she finally said. "We both acted stupid."

"Maybe, but I think I was way more stupid than you. And I am so sorry, Mel. I know it's a lot to ask, but do you think you could find it in your heart to give me one more chance? I swear I'll get it right this time." He took her free hand, relieved that she didn't pull away. "You know that I love you, right?"

She nodded.

"And you love me, too?"

She sighed deeply. "Of course I do."

"And you're going to give me another chance?"

She rolled her eyes. "Like I have a choice. I get the distinct feeling that you'll just keep stalking me until I say yes."

He grinned, thinking that she was probably right. "In that case, you could hug me now."

She cracked a smile and walked into his arms, and he wrapped them around her. Even with the grocery bag crushed between them, it was darned near perfect. *She* was perfect.

"You know, deep down I didn't really think it was over," she said. "I figured you would come around. And of course I would be forced to take you back. *Again*."

"But only after I groveled for a while?"

She grinned. "Of course."

He leaned down to kiss her, when a box sitting at the

very top of the grocery bag caught his eye. There's no way that was what he thought it was….

He pulled it out and read the label, then looked down at Mel. "A *pregnancy* test? What is this for?"

She was grinning up at him. "What do you think?"

He shook his head in amazement. *"Again?"*

"I don't know for sure yet. I'm only four or five days late. But my breasts are so tender I can barely touch them and that was a dead giveaway last time."

"I don't get it. I'm *supposed* to be sterile from the radiation."

"You might want to get that checked, because for a guy who is supposed to be sterile, you seem to have no problem knocking me up."

He laughed. "This is nuts. You realize that even if there are a few guys left in there, the odds of us going three years unprotected, then you getting pregnant not once but *twice,* is astronomical."

She shrugged. "I guess that just means it was meant to be. Our own little miracle."

He took the bag from her and set it on the ground so he could hug her properly. He didn't even care that people were driving by looking at them as if they were nuts.

As far as he was concerned, the real miracle was that he had let her go twice, and here she was back in his arms. And she could be damned sure he would never let her go again.

* * * * *

Don't miss the next KINGS OF THE BOARDROOM,
BACHELOR'S BOUGHT BRIDE
by Jennifer Lewis,
available May 11, 2010
from Silhouette Desire.

Harlequin Intrigue top author Delores Fossen presents a brand-new series of breathtaking romantic suspense!
TEXAS MATERNITY: HOSTAGES
The first installment available May 2010:
THE BABY'S GUARDIAN

Shaw cursed and hooked his arm around Sabrina.

Despite the urgency that the deadly gunfire created, he tried to be careful with her, and he took the brunt of the fall when he pulled her to the ground. His shoulder hit hard, but he held on tight to his gun so that it wouldn't be jarred from his hand.

Shaw didn't stop there. He crawled over Sabrina, sheltering her pregnant belly with his body, and he came up ready to return fire.

This was obviously a situation he'd wanted to avoid at all cost. He didn't want his baby in the middle of a fight with these armed fugitives, but when they fired that shot, they'd left him no choice. Now, the trick was to get Sabrina safely out of there.

"Get down," someone on the SWAT team yelled from the roof of the adjacent building.

Shaw did. He dropped lower, covering Sabrina as best he could.

There was another shot, but this one came from a rifleman on the SWAT team. Shaw didn't look up, but he heard the sound of glass being blown apart.

The shots continued, all coming from his men, which meant it might be time to try to get Sabrina to better cover. Shaw glanced at the front of the building.

So that Sabrina's pregnant belly wouldn't be smashed against the ground, Shaw eased off her and moved her to a sitting position so that her back was against the brick wall. They were close. Too close. And face-to-face.

He found himself staring right into those sea-green eyes.

How will Shaw get Sabrina out?
Follow the daring rescue and the heartbreaking
aftermath in THE BABY'S GUARDIAN
by Delores Fossen,
available May 2010 from Harlequin Intrigue.

HARLEQUIN® *Presents*®

Bestselling Harlequin Presents® author

Lynne Graham

introduces

VIRGIN ON HER WEDDING NIGHT

Valente Lorenzatto never forgave Caroline Hales's
abandonment of him at the altar. But now he's
made millions and claimed his aristocratic Venetian
birthright—and he's poised to get his revenge.
He'll ruin Caroline's family by buying out their
company and throwing them out of their mansion...
unless she agrees to give him the wedding night
she denied him five years ago....

Available May 2010
from Harlequin Presents!

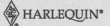

HARLEQUIN®

INTRIGUE®

BESTSELLING
HARLEQUIN INTRIGUE® AUTHOR

DELORES
FOSSEN

PRESENTS AN ALL-NEW
THRILLING TRILOGY

TEXAS MATERNITY:
HOSTAGES

When masked gunmen take over the maternity ward
at a San Antonio hospital, local cops, FBI and the scared
mothers can't figure out any possible motive. Before
long, secrets are revealed, and a city that has been on
edge since the siege began learns the truth behind the
negotiations and must deal with the fallout.

LOOK FOR

THE BABY'S GUARDIAN, *May*
DEVASTATING DADDY, *June*
THE MOMMY MYSTERY, *July*

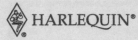
LAURA MARIE ALTOM

The Baby Twins

Stephanie Olmstead has her hands full raising her twin baby girls on her own. When she runs into old friend Brady Flynn, she's shocked to find herself suddenly attracted to the handsome airline pilot! Will this flyboy be the perfect daddy— or will he crash and burn?

Babies
&
Bachelors
USA

"LOVE, HOME & HAPPINESS"

Love Inspired

Former bad boy Sloan Hawkins is back in
Redemption, Oklahoma, to help keep his aunt's
cherished garden thriving and to reconnect with the
girl he left behind, Annie Markham. But when he
discovers his secret child—and that single mother
Annie never stopped loving him—he's determined
that a wedding will take place in the garden
nurtured by faith and love.

REDEMPTION
RIVER

Where healing flows...

Look for

The Wedding Garden
by Linda Goodnight

*Available May 2010
wherever you buy books.*

Steeple
Hill®
LI87595

HARLEQUIN
Ambassadors

Want to share your passion for reading Harlequin® Books?

Become a Harlequin Ambassador!

Harlequin Ambassadors are a group of passionate and well-connected readers who are willing to share their joy of reading Harlequin® books with family and friends.

You'll be sent all the tools you need to spark great conversation, including free books!

All we ask is that you share the romance with your friends and family!

You'll also be invited to have a say in new book ideas and exchange opinions with women just like you!

To see if you qualify* to be a Harlequin Ambassador, please visit www.HarlequinAmbassadors.com.

*Please note that not everyone who applies to be a Harlequin Ambassador will qualify. For more information please visit www.HarlequinAmbassadors.com.

Thank you for your participation.

BAP09BPA